THE RIDE II

"Final Resolution"

THE RIDE II

"Final Resolution"

LaRone Dyson

KB DESIGNS & PUBLISHING
2015

First Printing: 2015   UNITED STATES OF AMERICA

ISBN: 978-1-329-08135-2

KB DESIGNS & PUBLISHING
http://www.kbdesignsandpublishing.com

Ordering Information:

Special discounts are available on quantity purchases by corporations, associations, educators, and others. For details, contact the publisher at the above listed address.

U.S. trade bookstores and wholesalers, contact KB DESIGNS & PUBLISHING at (301) 643-5484 and by email at kbdesignsandpublishing@gmail.com.

Dedication

I would like to dedicate this book to my sons: Jason, Apollo and Justin. Watching you guys grow up to be a promising success, that you are today as men, makes any parent proud to say, "Yes, they are my Sons"! I know life was difficult with me not physically being there by your side while growing up. My deployments, while I was in the Navy, was a grave struggle for me too not being there with you; sharing the good and bad times. And to my late Grandmother Jennie Johnson (Grandma), your vision to see into my future was incredible; you said I would do it and I did. So this book, I dedicate to my sons and my Grandmother. I declare this book to be my legacy to you.

Contents

Acknowledgements

First, I'd like to give my very all and thanks to my Savior, Jesus Christ. Only through God, all and everything is possible.

Special extreme thanks to my Publisher and Editor, Mrs. Kisha M. Morris, for her supreme patience, relentless hours and days of unmeasured energy to putting this book together.

Shout out to my photographer, Thaddeus, for image and photography support. Your input for visual capture was indeed noted and praised.

Thank you, Tamira, for jumping right in on a short fuse notice in withstanding unbearable and unforgiving cold temperatures for modeling for the front cover of my novel. You were a true champion throughout the full four-hour photo shoot.

My parents, Eric and Barbara, from the very beginning, you both have inspired me to follow my dreams and never give up on anything I set out to do. You both fueled me to believe in myself to do what I desired to do or be no matter how big I dreamed; you both always encouraged me to put a plan to it and make it happen. I love you both. To my sister, LaShawn (Ms. Bossy), thank you for being that safety net for when I needed it the most, love you.

Thanks to my Aunt Theresa and Uncle Ronnie. You were and always will be my home away from home. You listened with your hearts and embraced me with your unconditional love.

Special thanks to my cousin, Damon C., to whom started and created the original RIDE GENRE "THE RIDE I". He challenged me to write the sequel "THE RIDE II: FINAL RESOLUTION". Thanks for all your support. We will fly to the stars with this one.

To my cousin, Nijila D., who pushed me to get the book finished and in the hands of hungry readers. You have truly inspired me to believe my story is worth getting out there.

My cousin Janae S. (Big Sis), all my love to you, since I returned home from the military, you have supported me through hardest of times during my transition into the civilian sector. Thank you for believing in my dream to bring this vision to life. All my love and heart to you.

My cousin, Barry W. and Alvin L, through the 35 years of time; we kept it real with who we are and have never forgotten where we came from.

My greatest nephew, James "LJ", I am truly proud to see the challenges you have taken on and never let up to achieve your goals.

To my guiding lights in the Navy, my Navy brother that started it all at my first duty station; USS IOWA (BB-61) David Smith, Operation Specialist Second Class. Blood, rust, sweat and tears is what forged us through our weight training routines, a tradition we still uphold today.

Darren Smith, author of the book "HOW TO STAY MARRIED FOR AT LEAST 100 YEARS"; Lloyd Coore, Lieutenant Commander, United States Navy; James Brown, Lieutenant Commander, United States Navy (Retired); and Wallace Robison, Chief Warrant Officer 4, United States Navy; Christopher Birl Quarter Master Senior Chief (Retired) Algernon Shaw, Operations Specialist Chief (Retired), United States Navy; and Thurman Norman, Quarter Master First Class (Retired), United States Navy. While stationed in Bahrain with you guys, words cannot alone thank you for all the professional, personal advice and guidance while going through life's challenging and changing experiences. You never judged me and you always kept me challenged to accomplish personal goals I set for myself.

A shout out to my gate keepers at NAVCOMTEL STA, Sigonella. My last duty station 2004-2007. G. Mason, Information Technician First Class, you are the solid symbol of structure and coordination. Christopher Jones, Information Technician, First Class, thanks, Jones, for your genuine integrity to keep our department true to its point. T. Naylor, Information Technician, First Class, your dedication to ensure mission accomplishments was recognized and applauded. S. Washington, Information Technician, Second Class, being a single parent, you gave no excuses requiring your presence at a moment's notice.

My Godbrothers, Tony and Jeffery Ross, you guys have shown me nothing but brotherly love since we were kids, and may God bless your mother's heart Ms. Ross. Thank you, Ms. Ross, for taking me in as your own.

To my Corvette Club Brothers: Donta, Mark, Reggie, Bae, Mitch and William, you guys never let me lose sight of me turning my dreams into a reality. And we are just warming up.

Many thanks to Kevin L. and Mike J. for moving mountains I had trouble moving.

A special thanks to the Holt family, Ms. Margret (Ma), John, Michael, Timothy, Theresa and Cynthia for all your support and the fun family trips. Highly looking forward to another Myrtle Beach adventure!

My Lady Best Friends for Life, Margie J -Thanks for your faith and believing in my dream to one day compete in bodybuilding since the age of 14; Aprile C.- my first client and as your Personal Trainer and personal dear friend, thank you for keeping it real in and out the gym; Zina W. and Marsha J.- I know I can surely count you both when I need a good laugh for the day, thanks for keeping me smiling; Tyra R.- thanks for including me in on all your outgoing activities, you never skipped a beat; LaToya J.-Congrats on your satisfied journey to happiness, you deserve the best; Gail M.-Through your challenging times you always kept a positive attitude and found time to check in on me.

And to the professors of Strayer University: Math Professor, Cedric Harris; English Professor, Jà Hon Vance, Strayer University Owings Mills Campus Department of English and Humanities; Psychology Professor, J. Wood and Business Professor, Milton Lawler; Ph.D. President, Ashante Fe Education. Your encouragement not to limit myself and to further my education has opened many doors. Thank you again.

Foreword

The power of words can move you to tears and evoke absolute joy or lead you into action. "The Ride II" had taken me straight to action. Every page turned leaves you on the edge of your seat wanting to know why and when. It has absolutely captured the streets of Baltimore in every aspect. Ivy is a force to be reckoned with.

-Tamira G.

"The Ride II: Final Resolution" offers another true view of life on Baltimore streets. Ivy sheds light on B' More's, "Get mine's first, all other's second" mentality. Hopefully her ending was a blessing for a beginning. LaRone's depictions of Baltimore's street life animates the existence and determination to survive "Street Life". "The Ride II: Final Resolution" is powerful, deeply moving with penetrating passion from each character.

- Nijila D.

Read the story and it was awesome; true to its origin. I'm a motorcycle enthusiast and the story was great. Looking forward to seeing more work from LaRone.

- Damon C.

The story is inspirational... because it tells you no matter what you're going through or how you're living, guns and violence isn't the answer; there's always a peaceful ending somewhere.

- Karen D.

Masterly minded and well put together, every page takes you on a ride to anticipation in rewarding it with suspense and excitement. I just couldn't read one page and put it down. The events of the story are guaranteed to put you right in the mist of the action and cheering for victory.

- Kevin L.

For the love of money is the root to all evil. This story gives you the clear definition of that cliché'. It also has a turn of events that are shockingly "Kool"; it goes to show you, that it's strength in numbers. Thanks for the story, Chief, it was awesome.

- Charelle L.

Preface

I was born and raised in Baltimore, Maryland in the North West district of Baltimore. I graduated from Northwestern High School in 1982. During my high school days, my parents geared me for the world in making two life changing decisions when I graduate from High School; either go to college and obtain a part time job or go join the military. Well that was simply a no brainer for me. I barely survived academics in school, so why would I set myself up for failure to go back to school? After I graduated, I proudly marched myself to the Navy recruiter in downtown Baltimore on Howard Street which is no longer there and signed up for the Navy.

I was recruited and shipped off to basic training in Great Lakes, Illinois, May 10, 1983. And here's the funny part, guess what, people? The Navy sends you to school while in basic training, retired from the Navy May 2007.

I am currently an alumni student at Strayer University, just two semesters shy in obtaining my Bachelor's Degree. Should all go well, I will be graduating with my Bachelor's in December 2015.

The real story behind "The Ride II: Final Resolution" was originally screen written by me and was arranged to become a movie. The origin of "THE RIDE" was written and directed by Damon Chambers (my cousin) in association with Libra House Films. I showed a great interest to become a part of this magnificent project while "The Ride I" was in production.

Damon recruited my assistance due to my keen since of attention to detail.

While reviewing the script, I pointed out to him that I could write a sequel to "THE RIDE I" based on one line I read. He replied with a huge grin "Really?" and added "Ok, go for it. I want to see what you got". I began writing in October of 2006, seven days a week for six months my pen didn't rest nor did I, the script was finished in March 2007. Although the first "RIDE I" didn't quite make it off the ground due to lack of funding and staff support, we began shooting "THE RIDE II: Final Resolution" in July 2007. Fate repeated itself again, like the first movie, "THE RIDE I" and tainted our confidence to finish it; therefore, we were forced to shut it down.

The script for "THE RIDE II: Final Resolution" stayed in dormant for eight years. One day I was looking in my closet, reaching for something else and a binder fell down instead. It was the script for "THE RIDE II: Final Resolution". I retrieved it from the floor and opened it one page at a time and had flashbacks of the tough times my cousin and I endured to get this off the ground. So I kept the script out to motivate myself back in the saddle in entertaining the thought of "maybe".

Several months ago in 2014, while I was sitting in class one night, a student colleague was at her desk. I couldn't help but to notice her ruffling through her huge purse looking for her text book and she pulled out a novel. She placed it on her desk while still looking for her text book. When I glanced at the novel, the idea hit me like a bolt of lightning. *Turn the movie into a novel.* I couldn't wait to go on break to share the idea to Damon. After explaining not only the "movie into a book idea" but I added even a more believable sales pitch to him. The revenue earned from "THE RIDE II: Final Resolution" novel could financially support its original idea of being a movie again. And there it is, also pending on the demand to want more, Damon and I are already ahead of you and discussing a possibility for him and I to write part three for the novel and produce a movie "THE RIDE III".

If you are reading this it only could mean one thing, that you purchased this novel. Therefore, I am sending you and everyone else a personal thank you; hoping you enjoy reading this story as much as I was excited the day I finished writing it.

Introduction

There are three sides to every story: your side, their side and the truth. Many times we want the outcome to fall in favor for benefits or profit; sometimes that sacrifice will cost a hefty price. This story will take you on a turbulent journey and deliver "Love, Loyalty and Greed" in its purest form and bring you back. Not to worry, I'm not going to spoil the fun for you but be prepared to go on "THE RIDE" of your life.

Baltimore City is the place where it all goes down. With hundreds of identified districts, Baltimore City has been dubbed "a city of neighborhoods", and has been more recently known as "Charm City", to go along with its older moniker of "The Monumental City" (coined by sixth President John Quincy Adams in 1827), and its more controversial 19th-century nickname of "Mobtown" which makes this story even more compelling. Speaking on the subject of "Mobtown", let me tell you about Nomad Green. Nomad is rough around the edges but quick and smart in the streets. He rides with his motorcycle club *"THE HELL RAISER'S"* and keeps up his own pride and joy – "The Island City Tattoo Shop" where the "baddest tattoos happen in town". He's got big dreams, like everyone else; to be successful, to be

The Ride II: Final Resolution

his own boss and working honestly to get what he deserves in life but somehow his dark past seems to find its way back to the present day to haunt his dream.

And talk about a "Hell Raiser"? Let me tell you about Storm Chambers. Dangerously hypnotic to the eyes, making men dance around her natural beauty, Storm could charm the pants off of any man and get away with it with no shame. Storm attracted drama everywhere she went. Her power and thrill came from engaging with men that had authority, money and street power in "Mobtown"; that's where you would find Storm on any given day. Storm was not impervious to falling in love but it was her wild side that couldn't be contained after marrying Andrew Chambers and in the end, became her demise.

Andrew's potential and passionate drive had everyone marveling at his success in being the founder, along with his best friend Anthony Johnson and co-owner of one of the largest real estate companies on the market, "DYMBERS REAL ESTATES". DYMBERS REAL ESTATES owns casinos and department stores along with streams of revenue from condominium and estate sales on the Annapolis waterfront. Andrew's consistent run-ins with the police as a teen youth was a sure ticket to him becoming a permanent resident in cell block H but shortly after the sudden death of Andrews's mother, his childhood best friend Anthony's, nicknamed Tony, family stepped in to raise and groom him into the man he is today.

19

Andrew Chambers excelled in the business of marketing and in 2012, was named the ""*Youngest Most Richest" Entrepreneur of the Year*" at the age of only 30. Although Andrew and Storm were married for just over a year, you would think that Storm had it all; prestige, power and luxury because of his success alone. You'd think that that was enough for Storm but again, we're talking about Storm and the only thing that was missing was grit and excitement. I mean, to come home to find Storm's belongings packed up and gone with a suitcase full of her husband's stolen company money in her possession, it was a sure way for her to find exactly what she's looking for and running back to the streets.

Although raised by her Aunt Sonyia, everyone thought that it was a guaranteed no brainer that Storm would not be a "statistic to society". I mean what do you expect with going back to her old "hood rat" ways and mentality, surrounding herself with the "HIGH ROLLAS", not to mention shacking up with the man who runs half the streets in Baltimore City. Storm knows "street" when she meets Deon Hilton, quickly recognizes his boldness and that he is "about his business" and plays house with Deon, better known as "D".

As time moves on, so does Storm as she just disappears as she just did to her dejected husband, Andrew, within 6 months. But "D" doesn't take her disappearance lightly. There's no love lost in his heart for Storm hearing that she's shown too much interest in his latest growing enterprise and had been rumored to have been seen with "Nomad", a street territory good guy contender but indeed a threat to "D's" drug trafficking operation. Nomad was known to be the "gatekeeper and guardian" of keeping his side of the territory "drug-free". Upon this discovery, "D" quickly scatters his men on the streets to "keep tabs" on Nomad and Storm's every move before moving in for the kill. And so it begins…The Ride II…

Chapter 1:
Awareness

As the sun rises brightly on a pleasant summer morning, it's Friday in the heart of Baltimore's Downtown Westside. The orange golden hue shines dauntingly in on Drew's bedroom window. Shifting through his impressive wardrobe, trying to find a dress shirt to match his finely pressed Calvin Klein suit jacket and pants, Andrew has no idea of what's just been revealed in the headlines.

"Good morning and welcome to News Break 7 WBCT-TV where we have just been informed of the apparent homicide of a woman that occurred in Eastside of the Baltimore that involved gun shots and killing identified male, Deon Hilton, Storm Chambers and Keith Sanders. Police do not have any leads on the homicide at this time. They are asking for your help to close this case. If you have any information, please call 555-1800," announces the anchorman.

"What the hell?" Andrew yells, getting dressed for work, in shock of watching the news of Storms murder.

Andrew jumps as the telephone rings. Catching a quick glance of his caller ID, Drew knows instantly who it is.

"Yeah, I know. Man, I'm watching it now," he answered with a stern hesitation and sighed. It felt like his breath was just knocked right out of him all at the same time in just one sucker punch gone wrong. How could this be happening to him right now? Why did she have to take his money and just disappear without any explanation?

"You thinking what I'm thinking?" Andrew's best friend Tony jolts his head in reaction to the news he just saw as well.

"Yeah, whoever put a bullet in Storm and her boyfriend "D" got free dibs on my $500,000.00," Drew tells Tony sternly.

"Or it could be just floating around out there somewhere, which puts us in a mandatory position to retrieve it. We don't need that kind of paper out there contributing to negative actions and outcomes," Tony suggests as a matter of fact.

"The last time I heard she ran off to Cali with "D" almost a year ago. "What was she doing back in town?" Andrew shakes his head in confusion and in disbelief.

"Storm could have been coming back in town to finish the job; to clean you out. I don't know but, at this point, it doesn't matter; they are both dead." Tony replies angrily and with a "good riddance" type of smirk.

"Hey man, watch it! She's still my wife," Drew interrupts obviously still upset to find out that his wife was now dead.

"Yeah, excuse me Bro. My bad. But Drew face it, when she married you I told you from day one she wasn't in love with you but in love with the things you gave her. And it became even clearer when she ran off with "D". I have had your back for over 10 years since we started this company and watched you get shafted repeatedly. It's time to take a stand and claim back what's yours," Tony yelled sharply into the telephone. He was determined to get his point across to Drew right at this moment. They had been as tight as thieves ever since Drew's Mother passed away and Tony's family took him in. Tony was not about to let his best friend go down the drain over this conniving and deceptive woman. They had too much at stake in their friendship and their business to allow that to crumble their enterprise.

"You think it was possible she was in trouble and trying to make her way back to me?" Drew, in a more settled tone, asks looking off into space, trying to put all this together in his head.

"Are you serious right now? Damn man, listen to yourself! Did you hear what I just said? Do I need to spell it out for you? Storm was not in love with you but with your money, Bro! And as for her reappearance in town, I don't know why the hell she was here but I am going to get to the bottom of this, once and for all. I still have eyes and ears out on the streets so let me do some digging around and get back to you on that," Tony blurts back in frustration.

Tony still could not believe what he had just heard. I mean, really? After all that has happened? Was Drew serious? What was it really that Storm had on him to make Drew still believe that Storm came back all of a sudden for him after she left town with "D"?

"Hey, Man, I thought we left that life behind us?" Drew sighs as he looks away down at the floor feeling shameful and withdrawn.

"Well it's time to shake off the dust and bring it back to make it work for us," Tony replies with assurance.

"Yeah, well I remember awhile back you promised that no one would get hurt and looked what happened!" Drew interrupts.

"Yeah, yeah, yeah, whatever! That was purely an accident. She lived, didn't she?" Tony snaps his comeback,

"Yeah, barely. Look Tony, I don't want no guns; just answers, who did it and I'll take care of the rest," Drew slams the phone down angrily pissed off at the situation at hand.

Drew had to pull himself together to finished getting ready for work which seemed to take an eternity compared to any normal Friday morning. Living in Columbia, Md had its benefits. Columbia, Md is about

30 minutes from the western portion of downtown Baltimore that includes Market Center and many of the newest developments in downtown Baltimore. It has increasingly become the preferred residential section of downtown. It is also home to the site of the "Superblock" project that will include hundreds of condos and apartments as well as a variety of retail and commercial space that are prime realty for Drew and Tony's new client list for DYMBERS REAL ESTATES company, which is exactly why Drew chose this location to live, work and play.

Chapter 2:
THE BRIEFING

Tony is in his corporate office seated on the edge of his desk, accompanied with his personal private henchmen giving them a "Situation Report".

"Alright fellas, it's no secret we all know Storm and "D" were found shot and my man Drew wants names associated with this action. Let's make this crystal clear: he's not after revenge." Tony walks over to look out the window and stares at the busy streets and states with solid concentration. "This has nothing to do with revenge at all, just answers and when you think you have something, call me first before making any moves. No violence! Just info. Got it? Can you do this and get it right the first time?"

Maurice feeling a little offended by Tony's remark and replies, "Yeah we got it! But you didn't have to go there; it wasn't our fault that that woman was hit by the car. Besides she was in the way." Tony in disbelief of his response replies, "In the way? How was she in the way when she was walking on the sidewalk?"

The henchmen leave the office and Tony shakes his head in confusion and says in a quiet tone, "Why do I keep these guys on my payroll?"

Tony's office phone rings and Drew tells him to take charge in his place for a meeting at 10 am and 2pm meeting because he's not going to be in today.

Chapter 3:
THE FLASHBACK

In a panic, Drew looks through Storm's old files and papers that were stowed away when she left him in hopes of finding her Aunt's address and phone number.

"Got it!" Drew sighs in relief as he finds her Aunt's address but with no phone number. Drew takes a drive to the county where Storm's Aunt lives. While en route, thoughts and visions of Storm and himself wallow around in his mind the whole drive there.

Drew approaches the drive way and stops. While placing his hands on the steering wheel, he takes a deep breath and exhales slowly to gather his thoughts. He looks in the mirror for a vanity check and gets out his car. He walks up the driveway and notices the door is slightly ajar and knocks on the door gently.

"Hello, is anyone home?" Drew yells as he knocks again harder with caution and at the same time pushes the door. He hears a slight weeping.

"Help me, please, I'm hurt!" An elderly woman's voice calls wearily from a short distance.

"I hear you. I'm here to help. Where are you?" Drew calls out as he rushes to follow the voice.

"I'm in the kitchen. Hurry, please!" the voice replies desperately.

Drew reacts quickly as he spots Storm's Aunt who looks as if she has fell off a step stool trying to reach for an item out of reach.

"Oh my God! It's you! Where'd you come from?" Storms Aunt's says as her face lights up in surprise and despair. She reaches out to hug Drew while he's assisting her to a nearby chair.

"Yes, it's been awhile, Andrew, I heard you had gone to the Bahamas to branch out your business!"

"Hello, Aunt Sonyia. Well, it didn't work out so I returned back home. I wasn't sure if you still lived here. Aunt Sonyia...I –," Aunt Sonyia interrupts, "I know...I know why you're here. You want to help lay her spirit to rest. You know when her Mother passed, I promised her while she lay on her death bed, that I would finish raising Storm and keep her safe from the evil in the streets," she says in a soft spoken voice.

"Storm came by here just before leaving for California some time ago. I told her she was going in way over her head and getting herself back too deep into the streets. I knew with Storm marrying you she was safe and that would have kept her away from that fast life; but it seemed to have found her any way."

"I still remember the first day we met." Drew glances at a photo portrait sitting on the end table of Storm.

"How could I forget? I was there." Aunt Sonyia follows up with a slight chuckle as they both begin to wander back to the first day it all began.

~~~~~~~~~~

"So as we discussed last week in our phone conversation, the benefits of this merger outweighs any possible risk," Drew states to a businessman sitting across from him as he begins to dine on his plated meal. As Drew continues to boast on company's advantages, his attention is quickly taken by the presence of Storm as she excuses herself from her conversation with her Aunt to use the Lady's room. Storm's Aunt takes notice of Drew's immediate attention to Storm immediately.

Drew, trying to stay focused on the meeting at hand but positions himself to better see Storm's return to the table. Drew, with great anticipation, fastens the pace of the meeting to make his acquaintance with Storm.

"Storm, that guy over there has been eyeing you since you got up and came back," her Aunt smiles chuckles to Storm.

"Aunt Sonyia, you are always trying to play cupid!" Laughing and shaking her head.

"Storm, you should have saw his eyes when you got up; he took one look at you and got mesmerized."

"Now Aunt Sonyia, I still haven't gotten over my last boyfriend."

"And that's the problem, you haven't gotten out to enjoy the beauties of Life. Besides, your last boyfriend was a stone cold hood rat."

"Here we go again! His name is Ray, Aunt Sonyia." Storm smirks.

"Ray, Jay and Say, whatever his name is, he was still trouble, having kids all over the place, constantly avoiding to pay child support and dodging the police, and last but not least, always never having a job and the list goes on. I'm not one to bring up the past, but I'm glad his caught up with him and now he's got 12 years behind bars to think about it. Storm," Aunt Sonyia reaches out to hold her hand, "you have so much going for you. Why do you keep-" Aunt Sonyia pauses sharply as she looks at Storm then refocuses behind Storm and smiles as Drew is standing directly behind her with a playful hushed smile.

"Storm, I think we have company."

"Excuse me Miss, I can take over holding her hand if you like."

"Are you referring to holding my Aunt's hand or mine?" Storm quickly looks up behind her with a look of an abrupt surprise and replies in a playful sarcasm sort of way.

Drew smiles charmingly, making his way around the table to view Storm eye to eye and formally introduces himself.

"My name is Andrew. Drew for short and you know what they say: a hand in need is a friend indeed."

"Well Drew that would depend on what that hand has in mind but I'm going to leave that one to rest." Storm grins as she returns the intro with an anticipated response.

"Well, you got me." Drew responds feeling slightly embarrassed.

"Oh, look, I've got some missed calls and my battery is almost dead. Let me go take care of these calls." Aunt Sonyia tells as she sits him down and pats him on the shoulder.

"Please keep my niece company 'til I get back." Storm shakes her head laughing softly.

"You know you set yourself up for that one," says Storm as Drew chuckles slightly.

"Yeah, I tend to have a bad habit of that," Drew says as he looks into Storms eyes and continues but in a more serious tone, "Always making a fool of myself trying to get to the things I want the most."

"Nice come back. OK, the lights on. You can stay for a minute." Storm responds with a big smile and nods as she's being drawn in to his charm.

~~~~~~~~~~

"Aunt Sonyia, did Storm have any close friends that I didn't know about or mention any one in particular when she came by?" Drew questions concerned, as he is jilted from his memory of the first time they met.

"No but strange you should mention that."

"Why?" Drew asked as he turns towards her more focused.

"There was a woman who just left here asking the same thing."

"What? How long ago? Did she tell you her name? Was she a cop?" Drew asks on high alert.

"She just left about 20 minutes ago. Drove a black flashy car. I don't think she was a cop; she sure didn't dress like one. She said she used to model with Storm some time ago and was an old friend of Storms. She said was in town attending a fashion show and was checking up on Storm to see if she wanted to go" Aunt Sonyia reminisced smiling, "you know Storm was a pretty model." Aunt Sonyia picks up a photo of Storm and sighs slightly with grief. "I forget the woman's name. I'm sorry, Drew."

"Hmmmm. That's OK! And that's all she said?" Drew responds as he looks away slightly and then refocuses back to Aunt Sonyia.

"Yeah that's it," Aunt Sonyia says concerned, "Drew, what's this all about? Was Storm in trouble? Am I in danger?"

"No, Aunt Sonyia, not at all, but if she comes by again, could you give her my contact info?" Drew says reassuringly as he pats her on the shoulder, calming her and handing her his business card.

"Sure Drew, no problem, I will be sure to do that," Aunt Sonyia warmly smiles as she gives Drew a tight embrace. Drew leaves her home looking around cautiously before getting into his car.

The Ride II: Final Resolution

Chapter 4:
Be on the Lookout

Tony coordinates a sweep of the city streets, by the company's hired henchmen, talking to all sorts of contacts from the homeless to street vendors working food and clothing stands for any and all information about the fashion show and who shot Storm. Meanwhile, Nomad's crew convenes to discuss the situation at hand.

"Aye, I called you guys here to drop the 411. Word has it on the streets, "check this", that some dude is looking to find out who shot Storm. I don't think these are cops. Watch your back fellas, be on the low-low," Nomad says as he stands in front of his crew.

"What! You gotta be kidd'n! Man, you and your brother are going to have to lay low, this dude is probably about all action and no talk," Speed interjects to Nomad. "Yeah, but it was all self-defense. Had I not pulled that trigger, I wouldn't be here," Nomad pleads as he defends his actions.

"Nomad, this dude ain't trying to hear that Peoples Court shit, he ain't Judge Brown! Sounds like this dude was really into Storm and may want retaliation, and then again, he may want to thank you for taking "D" and Storm out," Flash, Nomad's best friend, blurts out.

"Yo, whud up? OK. I'm on my way!" Nomad says as he answers his cell phone rings as everyone has a look of surprise on their face. Nomad slaps his cell phone shut.

"Yo, I gotta go to the hospital. My brother says the doctor needs to talk to me about an update on Ma's condition. Man, my funds are running low," sighs Nomad as he exhales and rubs his head preparing himself for the news.

"Hold on, I'm bouncing with you!" His other boy, Speed, says as he catches up to ride with Nomad. Flash takes over briefing the crew while Nomad and Speed leaves.

"Damn man, Nomad can't get a break! First, his brother gets a beat down from an unknown group of guys a few weeks ago, then he takes the heat with

Storm's drama, this dude is on the hunt, and now No-mad's mother diagnosed with Cancer! This shit does not add up! Yo, we need to come together and do some side-bar racing to raise money to help with some hospital bills. Y'all down?" says Flash as they all nod their heads in agreement, stick out their hand, ball it into a fist and lowers it.

"Yeah, I'm down! Yeah, let's do this."

Chapter 5:
INFORMANT

"I'm going to find out who did this to you, Storm," Drew says with love as he kneels at Storms grave site.

"You say this guy goes to this store," Devonte says as he points down the street for clarification, "all the time to play lottery, huh?" Devonte questions a trouble-maker on Pennsylvania Ave as he points him in a general direction of an individual that is notoriously known to know everything all the time.

"Yeah, I'm surprised you haven't run into him. He's about this tall with a short afro. His name is Chris, you sure u ain't 5-0?" the stranger tells him.

"Oh I'm sure," Devonte responds with confidence as he looks around consistently aware of his surroundings.

"I don't know, man, you all dressed and clean cut like you the men in black." Devonte slaps a 20-dollar bill in his hands.

"Thanks man, here's a little something for your time." Devonte walks toward the store and scopes it out and questions a few people hanging around that appear to be well versed with the daily activities in the immediate area. Devonte approaches the group with confidence.

"Excuse me, my man, can you help a brother out?" Devonte questions as he reaches out for further information.

"Yeah, but first you help us out," Thug responds as Devonte's survival instincts alarm him to expect the unexpected. Devonte shakes his head, takes his sunshades off and places them inside his suit jacket and says calmly,

"Hey look here, Bro, I didn't come here looking for trouble. I'm looking for someone."

"Well it looks like you found him," Kev says to Devonte in a sarcastic tone.

"Nahhh, you don't fit the description," Devonte smiles and shakes his head.

"Oooohhh man, look at the gear he wearing! How much y'all think we can cash in on that? What's that you wearing, Italian cut shoes?" the Thug's friend looks Devonte up and down. Devonte stares at his shoes explaining the fine quality using that as a distraction for what's about to come.

"You know your fashion well. You're actually right, they are Italian cut but tailor made," as the thugs stare, Devonte replies with, "want a closer look?" Devonte strikes with a front kick to Kev's stomach and with the same foot delivers a high side kick to the face of Kev's friend, pivots around with the other leg delivering a jaw breaking spinning kick to the other thug bringing him to the ground instantaneously. Devonte regains composer quickly to prevent more unwanted attention and helps one of the thugs up on his feet that's barely coherent, gripping the thug firmly by the back of his shirt.

"Now I tried to do this your way. Now let's do it my way. Is there someone by the name of Chris that plays the lottery here daily? Do you know him?" Devonte replies.

"Yeah, I know him. He comes by every afternoon and evening. Damn man, you didn't have to set it off like that, we were just having fun with you," Kev says still trying to catch his breath and bent over from having the wind knocked out of him.

"Really? For real! So was I, no love loss. Here's a little something for your troubles." Devonte tosses a $20-dollar bill on the ground in front of Kev and says, "All you had to do was simply ask "I'm a Democrat". Devonte looks at his watch and makes a phone call to his colleagues.

Chapter 6:
THE 411

Devonte then called his partners to meet up with him where he is now. Devonte looks at his watch and spots his compadres as they drive slowly by his car and gives them a quick gesture to find a parking space. As they walk towards Devonte, he gets out his car to meet them to shorten the distance of walking.

"Thanks for showing up," they give each other side handshakes, "here's the deal. There's a guy name Chris that plays the lottery daily and knows everybody and everything. He should be arriving about...now" Devonte looks at his watch and points at the front of the store and notices a man getting out of a car making his way into the store fitting the description given to him earlier.

"Alright fellas, let's move," Devonte yells calling the shots. All three henchmen walk swiftly across the street to meet with their potential informer. Devonte enters the store while his compadres wait outside. Devonte, this time, is more cautious of his approach and keeps an offset distance not to scare him off.

"Excuse me, Sir, could I buy a moment of your time?" Devonte says as he flashes a $50 bill. Chris looks around to make sure there's no misunderstanding for mistaken ID.

"Hell yeah," he says as he reaches for the money but Devonte pulls it away.

"It's yours and more where that came from if you can drop me some info on a woman by the name of Storm that was shot." The informant snatches the money from Devonte's hand and whispers, "Look here, we need to talk about this somewhere else. Meet me at Security Square Mall Food Court in 2hrs. Don't be late."

"We will be there," Devonte says as he follows Chris out the store.

"We who?" Chris says as he exits the store. He then notices the remaining two henchmen.

"Damn! Who the hell are you guys? What? Is the President in town or something?" he turns and says, "Remember 2hrs."

Chapter 7:
GOOD NEWS

Tony's cell phone ring and Devonte fills him in that he's getting close. Tony reminds Devonte not to make any sudden moves but just to ask questions. Nomad arrives at the hospital and is drawn in quickly by a nurse's beauty, winks and smile as he enters the elevator. As the elevators door closes, she returns the same as the doors close.

"Man, you just don't give up! Remember, it was thinking with the wrong head that got you in this mess with Storm in the first place," Speed says to Nomad shaking his head, while in elevator going up.

"And my brother, what head did Adam use before he bit that apple?" Nomad comes back.

"And that's my point! We are all paying for that now," Speed rapidly responds.

"Naaahhhh…not all of us," Nomad laughs shaking his head. The elevator door opens. Nomad takes in a deep breath, exhales slowly and prepares himself for the news from the Doctor. Nomad and Speed approaches his mother's room. Nomad enters the room and sees his Mother asleep, while his younger brother is sitting close by her side. Nomad greets his brother and Speed follows suit with the greet for Nomads brother. Nomad greets his mother with a kiss on the cheek. He then scans the room taking notice to the medical equipment used to facilitate his mother's status.

"How long has she been sleep?" Nomad quietly breaks the silence."

"She's been off and on. I think it's the medication." Ricky responds as he glances at their mother and turns back to Nomad. "How you hold'n up?"

"I'm good," Nomad looks around, "Where's the doctor?" Nomad replies. Ricky looks at his watch and looks away.

"Been gone for 15 min. He said he would be right back." Nomad focused on his brother.

"You said he wanted to talk to me? Do you know what this is all about?" Ricky looks at his brother.

"Yeah, but he can explain it better than me. Ma is doing okay though," Ricky says as the Doctor walks in with a smile and hearty greeting. Nomad turns and reaches out with his right hand to greet the doctor.

"Is she going to be alright Doc?" Nomad asks the doctor in a sensitive tone. The Doctor smiles and looks at his clip board making notes, "She's going to be fine," Nomad sighs with relief.

"Let me continue please. The cancer is in remission but as we ran more tests, we discovered her body is weakening from fighting this which as you can see she's consistently resting. If the cells continue to subside at this rate, she will recover and be home, however these particular cancerous cells have proven to cloak themselves in the past and with no warning at all and strike again." Nomad's expression reveals a look of trying to comprehend this data. "I know what your asking is, what does all this mean? Right?" Nomad's eyebrows clench together to brace himself for what's next.

"With your permission, we will need for her to stay here for a minimum of 3 weeks just to be sure. Also there was a medical breakthrough a couple years ago by a doctor in France that has developed a drug called "Androxtrophine" for patients recovering from this type of Cancer. She would take it twice a day for 6 weeks. The medication does have minimum side effects which makes it increasingly safe for her to take at this stage. Now for the bill, it is a high cost but it does work," the doctor tells Nomad and Ricky.

"It's all good, but I'm almost afraid to ask what's your meaning of high cost?" Nomad quotes with confidence.

"One week of prescription cost $7,000. This type of medication cannot be taken on and off, it must be continuous, and normally health insurance covers this," the doctor says as he takes a deep breath.

"She's already maxed out on her health coverage while being here. I've been taking up the rest of the slack on that," Nomad says looking over to his mother. Nomad looks up at the ceiling, inhales then exhales as he looks down at the floor. He then turns to the doctor, "Okay, set it up. I'll get the funds." The doctor nods a goodbye then turns around.

"I'm sorry, based on this situation, this is the best route to go." the doctor tells them as he departs the room.

"Man, where we going to get that kind of money? I got some ideas! But you may not like it!" Ricky says with concern.

"Nahhh, we don't have to go down that road, I fought too hard to keep you from following in my bad footsteps and besides Ma wouldn't be proud to hear that. Speaking of hearing, we don't need to be discussing this while she's sleep. Stay with her 'til she wakes up and tell her everything is going to be fine. She's going to be here a little longer than I anticipated but don't tell her that," Nomad tells Ricky shaking his head. Nomad gives his brother a hug and kisses his Mother on the cheek and whispers in her ear, "I know you can hear me. Ma, you have sacrificed your all in life to give us a chance now it's time for us to take care of you," Nomad looks up at the ceiling and takes a deep breath to hold back his hurt.

"Com'n, let's go." Nomad turns and leaves quickly. Speed is not liking what he sees in Nomad's demeanor while walking down the hallway.

"Yo man, I know that look in your eyes, what are you up to? Nomad voice becomes stern.

"Just stay close you'll see!"

Chapter 8:
RENDEZVOUS WITH INFORMANT

The informant, Chris, makes his way to the Food Court at Security Square Mall, looks around and spots Devonte accompanied by his compadres. Devonte offers the informant to sit and Chris accepts the invite.

"Fellas, fellas, so word has it, you guys out for the person that shot this Storm, huh?"

"No we're just looking for names to go with this action and that's it, no one gets hurt," Devonte reassures him.

"Oh, I get it, you get names and walk away and that's it, huh?" Chris says as he folds his arms and leans back with a sly smile.

"Yeah, that's it, and to mention you walk away with your account feeling quite happy," Devonte tells him as he opens his hands out. Chris gets to the point.

"What's the info worth to you "BIG TIME"? Chris looks to Jason who is getting impatient.

"OK, let's cut through the chase and tell us what you know!" The informant leans back and taunts and moors.

"Maybe!"

"Either you know or you don't! Our time is valuable here," the henchmen yell out looking at each other with a look of irritation. Maurice slides the informant $500.00 on the table.

"$500 up front and should your info check out legit, another $500.00 and our deal is done!"

"Y'all sure you ain't cops, because I be watching those movies like "The Wire", "The Shield" and "New York Under...," Devonte interrupts shaking his head.

"We're not who you think we are; we're on your side but operate on a higher level and that's all you need to know."

"OK, that works for me! Word has it that it was a party awhile back that Nomad hosted. He's associated with this motorcycle club called "Hell Raisers". Anyway, this big time drug dealer named "D" ran the West and East Coast but Baltimore was headquarters and safe for him. He called this home base. Anyway, "D" was associated with a bike club called "HIGH ROLLAS" and was trying to get close to Nomad to have him join him to move his product in his turf. But this Nomad dude was not trying to join him nor let him into his territory.

The whole conversation took place right at the spot where Nomad hosted his party. Right after the party, when his younger brother was about to get on his bike to head out, a couple of guys jumped him and hurt him pretty badly. No one knows if "D" had a part in that or not. Again, Nomad was not going along with "D"'s plan to allow him to bring his drug operation into Nomad's turf; he was not trying to have that.

So "D" devised a plan to use his woman "Storm" to get close to Nomad. Oh and man did she get close! Rumor had it she fell sweet to him and dropped "D" and that's when he set out looking for her and Nomad. "D" caught Storm alone and lured Nomad to come see him to talk and caught Nomad totally off guard holding Storm hostage with a piece to her head. And a big shoot out happened but no one is talking who shot Storm."

"So where do we find this Nomad?" Maurice asks the informant. The informant takes a deep breath.

"That's the hard part. Nomad moves around quite a bit; this guy never sits still. The club hosts a lot of bike races, you know for kicks and money. You might can find him at one of those. Aye, can a brother get a "Happy Meal" or something? All this talking making me hungry." The henchmen look at each other shaking their heads in disbelief of whether or not they should trust him.

"Can you find out when and where the next race is?" Maurice gestures.

"Can you get me a "Happy Meal"? Hell, it ain't even got to be happy just get me a meal and I'll be happy," Chris, the informant, gestures. Devonte looks at Maurice.

"Yo man, you got'em?"

"Hell no! I just gave him $500.00!" Maurice answers with a slight whine. Maurice looks over to Jason and he looks the other way, rubbing the back of his head not wanting to be bothered.

"Fellas, fellas! No need to fight over me, is this like y'all first date or something?" The informant jokes with a big smile.

Chapter 9:
DREAMSCAPE WITH STORM

Drew drives back into town and stops by a local eatery for a bite to eat and to absorb all that has taken place during the day. He sits down and looks around waiting for service.

"Good afternoon, Sir, can I interest you in a cup of coffee or tea?" The waitress says as she greets Drew and smiles. Drew returns the same displaying a bit of day time humor.

"No, but you can interest me in a shot of Vodka. The waitress laughs.

"I know right! We would be all feeling good around here!" the waitress replies jokingly with a hint of flirting. Drew admires the returned sense of humor, chuckles, then begins his order. While his food order is being prepared, Drew gets up to glance at the magazine rack to kill time. Browsing through the magazines, he notices a poster outside posted to a light pole advertising a fashion show Saturday at 7pm, calls the number for more info and then calls Tony.

"Yo, Drew, glad you called! Just got off the phone with my contacts. OK, here's the word on the streets. Not quite sure how this may tie in, but this guy, Nomad, bumped heads with "D" at some party a couple weeks ago. Strangely, shortly afterwards, Storm and "D"'s body was found dead. Again, not sure if there was some sort of connection, but the police still don't have any leads up to this point. However, it looks like we may have something if we can find this Nomad cat. I'm turning over a couple rocks now to find his hangout." Tony says sounding upbeat.

"That's pretty good. Thanks. As for this fashion show, I will be going to see what I can turn up there," Drew says sounding pleased.

"I hear what you're saying, but listen to yourself; you don't even know what this woman that maybe there looks like, you're chasing a ghost. Look, I'll come by the house and compare more notes to see what we can dig up. Meanwhile take a chill and get some rest," Tony says placing logic. Drew realizes the truth and agrees.

"Yeah, your right. I'll do that! Thanks again," Drew says as he pulls up in the driveway into the garage. The garage door remains open while Drew gets out to retrieve his daily newspaper. He waves a friendly greeting to a couple of admiring female neighbors. He makes his way into the house and while opening the paper, the fashion show flyer is dropped to the floor. He quickly retrieves it and with a quick glance, smiles and shakes his head. Then he makes his way in the kitchen tossing the paper on the kitchen counter along with the flyer.

Drew retrieves a bottle of Vodka along with a glass and the fashion show flyer. Drew makes his way upstairs to his bedroom. He sets the bottle and glass on his night stand and reaches over to his answering machine to retrieve messages from his phone. As the messages are heard, Drew loosens his tie and shirt in the mirror and with a look of relief, he turns on his lamp on the night stand. Drew sits on the side of his bed and reaches for the fashion show flyer, studies it while taking shots of Vodka. Numerous shots of Vodka. Drew glances over pictures of Storm and himself together and finally passes out on the bed.

~   ~

Awakened by water being run in the shower in the bathroom, still feeling hazy, he struggles to pull himself together to focus on the activities going on in the room. Drew finally gets on his feet and approaches the bathroom with a look of serious confusion. He slightly pushes the door open to get a strategic peak and to his utmost heart dropping surprise, reveals the impossible "Storm" taking a shower. Now even more confused, Drew can't tell reality from fantasy. Drew approaches with caution, walking very quietly and slowly to get a closer look, like a predator to his prey, while approaching the shower.

Drew almost begins to emotionally break.

"Storm?" Drew questions as he views Storm from the back taking a shower through highly blurred distorted glass as she turns around sounding happy.

"Oh, hey Baby! I've been wondering how long you were going to be. How was your meeting?"

"What meeting? What's going on here?" Drew asks Storm in total confusion.

"They said you were," Drew pauses, "...dead!"

"Drew, stop playing! As you can see, I'm right here. Baby, hand me that towel," Storm replies smiling. Drew hands her the towel and assists in wrapping it around her from behind along with his arms wrapping her in the front.

"You know I missed you today."

"Baby, I've been missing you for a long time."

Drew still behind her with arms wrapped around her, begins kissing her on her bare shoulders and neck. Storm reaches from behind and begins to massage the back of Drew's head while she is enjoying his soft lips massaging the side of her neck. She throws her head up and back for him to gain easy access to the other side. Drew lifts Storm, mimicking a newlywed couple carrying his bride over a threshold. He makes his way to the bedroom and gently lays her down on the bed and covers himself on top of her. The moment heats up as she moans softly as she begins to reach her climax. The moans began to get louder as she starts to reach her peak and a loud pitch from her voice is released.

~   ~

Drew startled, jumps up from the sound of the phone; his heart racing and eyes bulging along with trillions of neutrons racing through his brain and his concentration is trying to become one.

"HELLO? HELLO?"

"Drew, it's Tony, you okay man?"

"Yeah, why, what's up? Drew squints and wipes his eyes still trying to focus.

"Man, I've been calling on your cell and home phone and you didn't pick up! You sure you okay, Bro?" Drew glances at the clock again wiping his eyes looking around still disorientated from the dream, peeking into his bathroom with caution while trying to convince Tony he's fine.

"Yeah, man. I'm alright. What's up?"

"Look, I just had something come up I need to take care of. I'm going to have to catch up with you at the fashion show tomorrow night," Tony tells Drew sounding convinced.

"Okay cool, no problem. I'll see you when you get there. Have you found out anything new?" Drew asks him in a calm tone.

"Naahhhh, not yet, but my boys will be out and about at first light tomorrow morning," confirms Tony sounding confident.

"Okay cool. Oh and Tony?"

"Yeah?"

"Keep it quiet. If word gets out that we are on a treasure hunt, all hell will break loose and no one will talk," Drew tells Tony.

"Yeah I know; don't worry we'll find it. Get some sleep. We have a long day ahead of us tomorrow."

Chapter 10:
IVY'S PLAN

The captivating view of the sunrise in Downtown Baltimore on a Saturday morning would ease any unwanted tension away. From the skyline of the Hilton, a luxurious high rise hotel, a woman wrapped in a towel making her way to answer the phone, eases her way into the room. She answers and sits down on the bed.

"Hello?" Ivy answers sweetly.

"Hey, just checking on you. Are you doing okay?" Her boyfriend Brian replies. Ivy chuckles softly.

"I called yesterday, Brian, to let you know I made it in town and you're just getting back to me?"

"Yeah, I know, my bad, I had some..."

"Look, I don't want to hear your sorry ass excuses. We owe big names a lot of money and promised to get it back to them. Time is of the essence here. I need for you to be a lot more attentive to what I'm trying to do here. Remember? I've got my ass on the line here for both of us," Ivy interrupts.

"You're right, Baby, and I'm sorry, it won't happen again," Brian explains sounding remorseful.

"Damn right, it won't happen again! You pull this shit one more time and I'll leave your ass out to dry and

---

then haul ass with the paper. You got it?" Ivy scorns. Brian adheres to her warning.

"Yeah I got it!"

"Good!" Ivy acknowledges.

"Did you find Storm?"   Brian asks Ivy, sounding concerned. Ivy softens her tone and exhales.

"No. I got to her too late. Storm was killed."

"What! How? When?"   Brian asks surprised.

"Her Aunt said she was shot last week. She said the police had no leads which also explains why she didn't respond to my text messages'" Ivy explains softly. Brian goes into a slight panic.

"Damn! She was our key to getting us out of this mess. What else did her Aunt say?" Ivy is frustrated.

"Nothing, her old ass didn't know shit! I know we both were banking on her getting us out of this. I should have broke camp when I received her first text for me to come to Baltimore to rescue her but I couldn't get away at that time. It looks like the plan has changed now. I'm going to have to go long and deep on this one; it's too much riding on this."

"Is there anything I can do from here to help you out? Brian tells her trying to help. Ivy lashes out at her boyfriend.
"Brian, you're all the way down in Florida! How the hell can you help me?"

"We are in this together, remember?"

"I'm sorry, I didn't mean to snap at you. Look, if you want to help, help me think this thing through."

"Now that's my Ivy talking."

"Damn it! Now that the plan has taken more than a slight turn, it's going to require a little more energy than I what I have time for. WAIT A MINUTE!" Ivy gains momentum, quickly locates her laptop computer case, opens up her computer and reviews the emails sent from Storm to gain a few points for clues. Brian questions Ivy's activity.

"Ivy, what are you talking about doing? What are you doing? Ivy explains to Brian while multi-tasking.

"I'm reviewing the email trail. She made mention of a motorcycle club she was in," Ivy says as her finger scans the email, picking out clues to aid her finding a point of contact, "called High Rollers but she started kicking it with this guy name Nomad and he was in a motorcycle club called Hell Raisers. I'm thinking if she got close to him, he can tell us about the money."

"Yeah that all sounds good, but how you gonna find this Nomad guy?" Brian asks Ivy jumping onboard. Ivy gets excited.

"I'm already on it," Ivy says while typing the name of the motorcycle club on the internet and the *Hell Raiser's* website appears. She claps her hand and rubs them together, "I gotta go."

"Be careful, Ivy, remember you're in uncharted territory up there," Brian offers advice to Ivy, "If the risk outweighs the outcome, just cancel out and come back. We will think of another plan to pay back this 200 grand."

"Man, are you crazy? You think I would drive all the way here to Baltimore and leave with nothing. Speaking of coming back, have they noticed my absence?" Ivy's reminds Brian of her quest. Brian gives Ivy assurance.

"No, not yet, but hurry and do what you gotta do and do it fast. They gave us a deadline of a week ago to have the funds paid in full. It's now going into week two, it's making me nervous, eyes are staring and ears are opening…"

Ivy interrupts, "Yeah, I know what comes next; fingers start pointing and bullets start flying. Look, just keep them off balanced for a couple days. I'll find this Nomad and the money and we will be out of this mess. Besides I have back up plan. Call me on my cell. I'll be at the fashion show tonight.

"Fashion show? I'm down here looking over my shoulder on every turn to avoid a bullet with my name on it and you're going to a damn fashion show?" Brian questions Ivy's comment.
"When are you going to learn to trust me? The fashion show is part of my back up plan," Ivy affirms.

"Yeeeeaahhh, you did make mention of a backup plan before you left. What is this back up plan and who…?"

"Gotta go. Sweety, I'll call if anything turns up." Ivy hangs up the phone quickly and stares at the *Hell Raiser's* website and begins surfing it for contact and activity info. She clicks on members and a group photo and Nomad appears in it.

"Gotcha now, which one of you is Nomad?" Ivy chants in a soft tone. Then she clicks on upcoming events and the website reveals a race being held at the race track Sunday at 4pm. She clicks back to the group picture and in a continuous soft tone she says, "Hmmm. Looks like it's going to be an eventful weekend."

Chapter 11:
THE PREPARATION

Andrew is sprawled out on the bed face down with his head to the side. With one eye opened, he is awakened by the neighbor's electric lawn mower. He conducts a visual survey, his hand reaches to rub his forehead and eyes. His mind is summoning the body to rise. He rolls over on his back very slowly. While lying on his back, with both hands, he grabs his forehead and sighs a low moan. Andrew turns his head to get a time check and then groans even more when discovering how much of the morning was slept away. He wills the energy to his arm and shoulder for support to sit up in a laying side position. He slowly rotates his legs to make way for both feet to touch the floor. Repeating the same "rubbing the forehead and eyes" ritual while sitting on the bed, he focuses on his bathroom door and begins having flashbacks of his dream and shakes it off. He finally gathers the strength to head to the shower.

While taking a shower, the phone rings. He hears it and decides to listen for the answering machine to pick up.

"Yo Drew, this is your boy, Rob from the shop. Pick up if you're there? Just reminding you of your 11 o'clock appointment. Be there. I'll holla! Peace."

"I hear you, Rob. I'll be there, partner." Drew responds out loud. Drew thinks to himself.

"Man, forgot all about that."

~   ~

Meanwhile, Ivy is looking at her GPS for directions to the fashion show. She's getting frustrated with traffic and missing turns because her GPS is not registering the address she placed in. She pulls over and asks for assistance from a pedestrian and shows him the address. He points her in the right direction. Ivy blows the horn and lowers the passenger side window to wave her hand getting the attention of a man standing on the corner on the cell phone.

"Excuse me, Sir, I'm a little lost. Can you help a sista out of a jam here?" He walks over to the Corvette's passenger side, bends down slightly to get a closer look inside the car and smiles taking another type interest to her.

"Damn, Baby, you rolling! Today must be my lucky day! Sista-Sista, you in a jam? Baby I got the peanut butter for us to make one hell of a sandwich."

"Yeah I bet you do. Look, I'm looking for this address. Can you help me?" Ivy questions as she displays a nonchalant smirk and hands him the directions.

"Yeah sure, Baby Girl, let me see what you got?" He asks as he retrieves it from her. The informant stands straight up and looks around to get his bearings.

"You must be from outta town. Yeah, this is where that fashion show is," he nods with a smile, "OK, pretty

Lady, you gonna go down 2 lights and make a right on Greenmount then follow that 'til it turns into St Paul and it should be on your right. You can't miss it. But it don't kick off 'til tonight. You're a little early, aren't you?" He asks as he hands her back the directions.

"Yeah, like you mentioned, I'm not from here so I didn't want to get lost trying to find it later on," Ivy says, as a matter of fact, as she retrieves the flyer and lets him know she's all business, "Thank you." Ivy rolls up the window. The informant steps back with a glad to help gesture.

"No problem, Baby. Aye, looky here," the window stops at a partial, "what does a brother gotta do to be with a fine woman like you?"

"First, be a gentleman! Second come up with better lines. Your shit is old, Daddy," Ivy says as the window is being raised. As the car takes off, he yells.

"Oh it's like that huh? That's alright! Aye, if you get lost come back and we can go find it together," he utters to himself. "Damn girl, you fine!" the informant says. As he watches the car leave, he takes out his cell phone to make a call. Devonte just exiting a store, reaches for his cell phone as it rings just before getting in the car.

"What you got for me? Alright, listen up…. The "Hell Raisers" are holding a bike race at the track tomorrow at 4pm and the stakes are high. I'm talking big time money."

"Will Noman be there?" Devonte inquires.

"His name is Nomad; you know you need to develop better listening skills. Hell yeah, he'll be there; he lives for this kinda shit, he gets off on it, he's like aaaahhh, watcha call one of them adrenaline junkies," the informant replies getting a little irritated.

"Good heads up! Thanks...." Devonte responds pleased as the informant interrupts.

"Whoa-Whoa-Whoa! Wait...," Devonte interrupts, "Don't worry, you'll get your money."

"No-no-no, that's just part of it! Word on the streets has it that Nomad's Mother is in Good Samaritan Hospital with some type of Cancer, so if you can't find him nowhere else, he'll be there." the informant implies. Devonte's wheels start turning,

"Mother in the hospital, huh? Tell me where to meet you to seal our deal."

"Cool! I'm down here on the corner of Franklin and Market. Hurry up, man, I need to get my numbers in."

Chapter 12:
THE INFORMANT
SCORES

Devonte is sealing the deal with the informant sitting in the passenger seat of the car. As he is counting aloud each fifty-dollar bill, when done, they shake hands and the informant departs the car. While shutting the car door, the informant bids his farewell.

"Nice doing business with you guys."

"Yeah, thanks again for pulling through." Devonte makes the phone call to Tony and he picks up. Devonte is anxious to reveal the news.

"You're gonna love this! There is a big bike race scheduled tomorrow at the track at 4pm and its guaranteed Nomad will be there."

"Good! Be sure to scope it 'til Drew and I get there." Devonte releases additional information.

"Got it! Also just got word that Nomad's mother is in the hospital with Cancer." Tony can't believe the news he's getting.

"Man talk about checkmate," Tony pauses.

"Hey man you still there?" Tony responds, "Yeah, you know what, Devonte, the price just went up. Call your boys and meet me in the conference room in an hour. I'll make some calls to the hospital to confirm this. Devonte looks at his watch.

"Got it." Devonte confirms as he puts his cell phone up.

~   ~

Drew pulls up in front of the Barber shop. Drew walks into the Barber floor and is quickly greeted by his favorite Barber nicknamed "Rob". They exchange the ritual hand and hug shake. The barber smiles with hands waving in gestures.

"What's up, man? I almost had to cancel you out. I didn't think you were going to make it." Drew makes his way to the barber chair.

"My bad Rob, I tried to call you to let you know I was going to be running a little late but your line stayed busy." Rob swings Drew around draping the traditional barber cape.

"Yeah Dawg, everybody setting appointments to getting it right for this Fashion Show tonight."

"This Fashion Show is a real big thing huh?" Drew inquires as his Barber is prepping his equipment.

"Yep, it's being hosted by this well-known designer "Ti'arra M" and she brings her new designs in town once a year before it hits the racks," Rob fills Drew in, "Her designs is off the hook and so are her after parties! The girls here at the shop are still talking about the last one she gave," Rob says as he begins to edge up Drew's goatee.

"Man, it's that serious? A Fashion Show?"

Rob assures him, "It's that...."

"I'm sorry man, let me get this," Drew tells Rob as he reaches for his cell phone. Rob backs off and steps away.

"What's up, Tony? Drew, my boys are on it. They found out info on the race and you ready for this? Nomad's mother is in the hospital with cancer.

"Really?" Drew responds, surprised with the detailed news.

"Sad to say, yeah, you know what else? Instead of us going to him, I came up with an idea to have him come to us," Tony tells him. Drew looks around and signals the Barber one more minute as he quickly removes himself from the barber chair to find a more private area to talk.

"OK. Tony listen, I don't want this guy to get hurt nor scare him off; we are getting close."

"Don't worry, Drew, I got this. Either he'll lead us to the money or lead us to who has it," Tony tells Drew sounding confident.

"My gut feeling is telling me your idea is not a good one but I don't have the time to argue based on what's at hand. What I can't figure out is how the woman that

was at Storm's Aunt house yesterday ties in with this?"
Drew tells Tony sounding a bit anxious.

"I don't know, but if we happen to single her out at
the show tonight, let's ask her," Tony says and chuckles
sarcastically.

"Look, I can't talk right now. I have to go but keep
me posted," Drew responds as he turns around signaling
his Barber that he's coming. Drew hangs up and apolo-
gizes to Rob for the delay.

Chapter 13:
A VISIT TO THE HOSPITAL

All is quiet as all three enter Good Samaritan and make their way to the elevator. Maurice breaks the silence while in elevator.

"Aye man, you think this plan will work with this guy Nomad? You know, make him surface? Jason smiles, nods and looks at Maurice, another of Tony's henchmen.

"It always does." Elevator door opens and the henchmen exit the elevator. They go into a visual scan mode. Jason turns his head and winks at the nurse working the desk as she checks him out from shoes to his head.

"Yo, here it is," Devonte whispers.

All three enter the room with high caution, carefully making their approach inside the room. Nomads Mother is still in a deep sleep as they all come to a halt. They all approach her bed and stare down at her. Maurice looks over at Jason.

"Are you sure this is her?"

"That's what Tony said, Room 219," Jason responds.

Jason scans for confirmation of identification. He lifts her wrist and reads the patient ID bracelet issued by the hospital and nods his head.

"It says it right here."

"Ok, let's hurry up and do this. Looks like she's waking up," Devonte whispers as Jason's reaches his hands inside his suit jacket.

Meanwhile, Nomad and his brother Ricky are making their way into the hospital lobby to the elevator.

"Man, you finally going to do it! My big brother owning his own business! *'Island City Tattoo Shop'.* It's good to hear good news for a change," Ricky, Nomads younger brother, proudly tells him.

"Yeah, it's been in the mix for a while, you know saving a little loot here and there. And when I got approved for that small business loan a week ago, I knew it was now or never," Nomad proudly smiles at his brother.

"Yeah, that was on time and on point. You been talking about doing this for a long time and it's finally happening." Ricky smiles and nods giving Nomad a side hand shake. The elevator door opens and they step in.

"Yeah now, I gotta do one more thing and everything will be everything."

"Oh yeah? What's that?" Ricky asks.

"Oh, your gonna love this! You'll see, Lil' Brother, just trust me," Nomad turns his head and smiles with a wink. Ricky jokingly throwing hand gestures all while playfully laughing.

"What? Make me an Assistant Boss Man? Run the register?

"Hell nahhh, you ain't running my register...remember you got fired at Wendy's for dipp'n into their register," Nomad playfully interrupts.

"Ah, that's cold! I...I was going to put it back. I was just giving myself a loan," Ricky says, not taking offence to his statement.

"You was going to put it back? How you gonna give yourself a loan with someone else's money without their permission?" Nomad asks and looks to his brother like a teacher to a student. The elevator doors open and they both exit and head toward their mother's room. Ricky explains.

"That's the part where I got caught up and," they both say together laughing, "and got caught!"

Nomad and Ricky make their way down the hallway still conversing. Just ahead, on the opposite side of the hallway, three silhouettes make their way towards them in passing. As Nomad and Ricky continue in their route, the closest point of approach has minimized the distance between him and the henchmen. Nomad has totally tuned out Ricky's voice and turns his head for a quick glance to Jason as he returns the same with a universal head nod. Nomad acknowledges and continues his route to his mother's room. The henchmen make their way to the elevator. Nomad and Ricky pause before entering the room. Ricky speaks in a low tone.

"Well, here we go," Nomad nods in agreement, "Yeah, here we go." A look of surprise on their face of what they can't believe they are seeing. Their mother is sitting up with a big smile looking at them anxiously wanting to hug them. They race to the bed to greet her. Ricky is the first one to greet her with a hug.

"Ma, you finally awake? How you feeling," Ricky asks holding her hand. Nomad's mother smiles and answers with a weak reply.

"I'm fine, baby, just tired that's all," their Mother says as she reaches out for Nomad's hand, "How's the man of the household doing?"

"I'm holding up. Speaking of up, we're glad to see your up. You were always sleep every time we came by to see you. The Doctor advised us to make our visit short with you so that you can get your rest," Nomad tells his Mother as he reaches to hold her hand.

"What's this?" Nomad asks as he takes notice of a rose and a card just next to his mother's leg.

"I don't know; I didn't even notice it there. Open the card and see who it's from," Nomad's mother responds.

Nomad opens the card and reads it to himself and a look of fury just comes over him. At that very moment, a flashback of images goes through his mind of Jason and Nomad exchanging a nod just moments ago passing each other in the hallway. He glances at his brother and races out the door and yells to Ricky.

"WATCH MA! I'LL BE RIGHT BACK!" Nomad races out of his Mother's room to the Nurse for quick exit information as the henchmen are in the elevator going down. Nomad races to the elevator and sees it in use and gets the attention of a staff worker by the arm requesting info for the location of stairs.

"QUICK! WHERE ARE YOUR STAIRS" He yells as he grabs her by the arm?

"HEY!" The nurse shouts as she is caught off guard and irritated, points, "down the end of the hall and make a left, you will see it."

Nomad jumps down the stairs three at a time with a quickness. As the henchmen reach their floor "L" for Lobby and door opens, they step out. Jason sees a bathroom and points to it.

"Hey, I'll be in here for a minute." He enters and the door it swings close. Devonte points to the gift shop.

"Alright, we'll be in here," Devonte says and he and Maurice enter the shop. Nomad finally reaches the Lobby. He tries to focus on people in passing but not fitting the henchmen's description. Just seconds before, Nomad makes his way to the closest exit and runs pass the restroom and Gift Shop. Nomad wastes no time reaching to open an exit door leading outside after feeling confident that he has covered the Lobby area.

Already out of breath, he rushes outside and goes into the parking lot to look for clues. His eyes scan the immediate area taking close notice to anything that may stand out. No clues are sighted and he heads back into the Hospital. Just as he enters the Lobby, his cell phone rings. Nomad answers the phone kneeled over out of breath.

"Hey Baby, what's up. Are you OK?" Nomad's girlfriend Sherri says disturbed.

"I'm fine. I should be asking you that!"

"What's wrong? Why are you sounding like that? You better not be get'n it on with some other girl! I will kick your ass!" Sherri barks as the signal breaks up. Nomad finds a private area heading back into the lobby hallway to regain a strong signal.

"Hell, nahhh!! Sherri. What's your damn problem girl?" Nomad yells, frustrated from her remark. He concentrates on his phone call with his back to the exit trying to maintain continuity for a phone signal. The henchmen engage in conversation as they exit the Lobby. As the henchmen make their way outside, Jason lowers his head slightly and reaches for the top bridge of his nose with his two fingers squenching his eyes. Devonte catches his movements.

"You alright man?" Jason sighs.

"I just don't like hospitals; they me make nervous." Maurice gives an attitude check to Jason.

"Hey man, don't go getting all sensitive and going soft on us now." Jason gives reason.

"Naaahhh, I've always had a phobia when it comes to doctors and hospitals," Jason tells Maurice as he goes hard, "Well, you need to shake it off and man up! We got a lot of work to do." As they get into the car, Jason and Maurice square off.

"Look, I said I'd be alright!" Jason snaps as he gets in the car. Devonte interrupts and fends for Jason.

"Damn, Maurice, he said he'll be alright. Why don't you leave him alone? Devonte gets into car. Maurice offended, he sounds off.

"I am, he just makes me uneasy talking like that; talking like he's getting that, what you call that shit them soldiers be coming home with when they zap out that, aahh…that uuuhh?" Maurice asks as he gets in on the driver's side of the car. Devonte interrupts him and finishes his sentence: "PTS". Maurice finishes his sentence.

"Yeah, that PTS shit, sounds like a venereal disease to me!" Maurice jokes as he starts the car and looks in the back seat to taunt Jason.

"Yeah, you got that PTS thing going on!" Maurice starts laughing, giving a playful high five to Jason. While Jason is giving him the middle finger, Maurice breaks his laughter, getting serious.

"What's wrong, Babyboy? I got nothing but love for you!" Maurice breaks out laughing again. Jason goes back to waving his middle finger.

"I don't know why you didn't join the Circus…you fuck'n clown! Just drive the car! I'm getting hungry." Maurice looks over to Devonte and laughs.

"Our boy is back."

Outside the hospital, two individuals make their way to the hospital entrance and walk into the Lobby and the hallway. Nomad looks up while still on the cell phone and recognizes the individuals. Nomad reaches out with the ritual hand and hug shake while still engaging in his conversation with his girlfriend. He gives them the hand gesture to wait one minute.

"Baby, look, I don't have time for this right now. My boys are here and I need to holla at them for a minute. I'll call you later," Nomad reassures her as he hangs up the phone.

"Yo, man, where'd y'all come from?" Speed speaks out first.

"Your brother called us and said you may need some help. Are you okay?"

"Yeah, I thought for a minute I would have, still looking around, but they left before I was able to catch them," Nomad tells them firmly. This confuses Flash.

"Them who? What are you talking about? Nomad takes a deep breath and begins walking to the elevator as they walk beside him and he explains.
"Check it, it seems someone knows something and wants me to break ice with them," Nomad tells them

discreetly as the elevator door opens and they all enter. Speed intervenes.

"Yeah, your brother was rambling on so fast about some card you read and then boom, the turbo kicked in and you was out!

"I'll let you see the card and then you will see why. It had a number on it, but when I read it something about it reflected the style of those three brothers Ricky and I passed while in the hall going to my mother's room earlier. I can tell it had their signature all over it."

"Speaking of your mother, how is she doing? Speed asks anxiously. Nomad smiles heartily.

"She's good. She's awake and everything," he tells Speed and as the elevator doors open they all exit.

"Yeah, Ricky's in there now talking to her." As they walk down the hall, getting closer to the room, Nomad notices a lot of activity just outside the room.

"What the hell! Nomad exclaims as he runs down the hall to see what's going on. He makes his entrance and his eyes can't believe what he's seeing; doctors and nurses are attending to his mother's now critical condition. Ricky, in tears, shoves Nomad out of the room to keep him from feeling more grief than already endured. The door closes behind them. Ricky screams to Nomad.

"NO, DON'T COME IN! LET THEM WORK ON

HER! LET THEM DO THEIR JOB!" Nomad tries to use his weight to out bulldoze his brother but his friends assist Ricky in restraining him.

"WHAT THE HELL IS GOING ON? LET ME GO! I WANT TO SEE HER!

Ricky forces Nomad back and yells at him.

"NO! NOT LIKE THIS!" Nomad's eyes now flood with tears and his friends are holding him trying to talk some sense for him to stand down and let the doctors do their job.

"LET ME GO MAN!" Nomad insists as Speed takes over.

"NOMAD, GET A GRIP! GO WITH US MAN! LET'S GET OUT OF HERE!" Speed gives Nomad a tight side hug and gets him to walk opposite way of his mother's room. Nomad, now wearing down and trying to regain his composer.

"I just wanted to see her..." He tells them softly as they walk away. Ricky signals to Speed and Flash that he's staying and will meet up with them in a minute and to attend to Nomad. Nomad walks away with Speed and Flash with visions of doctors and nurses still working on his mother.

Chapter 14:
THE CALL FROM THE DOCTOR

Nomad is accompanied by Speed on his motorcycle riding behind him departing the hospital parking lot. Flash, while mounting the motorcycle, makes a phone call on his cell.

"YO, call the boys and meet us at the clubhouse. We just went 'Code Red', I'll explain it to you when y'all get there. Flash closes his cell phone and catches up with Nomad with Ricky in following a full eye view of motorcycles pull up in the driveway and views them all unmounting motorcycles. All is quiet as they make their entry into the Clubhouse. The silence is then broken when Nomad enters the room and is greeted by his members with the ritual hand and hug greeting.

"Yo, man, when we heard what happened, we got down here right away. You alright?" a fellow club member asks in a concerned tone. Nomad nods his head, walks toward the chair and drops his helmet on the floor. He looks up, exhales and drops back in the chair rubbing his head.

"Thanks man. Talk about having one hell of day."

"Shit, this is all fucked up," another member responds.

"I know, man, tell me about it."

Ricky looks at his friends then looks to Nomad.

"We'll be alright; we've been through worst. RIGHT?" Nomad responds with a nod then Flash breaks the silence and claps hands together.

"Alright, listen up, Nomad got some heat coming down on him from somebody ----we don't know who, what, or why. It's important right now for us to stay close and keep each other safe. Most importantly, listen to the streets and what they say; we can't take this lightly. If a fly shits, I want to know about it."

"Yo, we need to take some Karate or boxing or something, so we can kick some ass," a third club member mimics' karate skills, then mimics a boxer. Other members watch him with a look of "you can't be serious" and irritation falls upon the group. They all chip in with at the same time.

"You so stupid! Shut up!" Speed chuckles slightly.

"Yo, you need to take a damn seat. You gonna get us all killed if you really fight like that...," Speed says as he shakes his head.

"Damn..." looks to his friend, "Go head, man, finish'" Flash comments as he gives the member a look of irritation.

"Anyway, as I was saying, we got to keep each other up on the 411."

"I was just trying to help," says first club member sounding offended.

"You want to help? How bout keep'n your mouth closed and your eyes and ears open," a fourth club member interjects. Flash shakes his head and smiles.

"I couldn't have put it clearer than that." Battle of the wits begin to stir up the air as Nomad friends begin clowning the rowdy member. Nomads' cell phone rings. He takes it out and notices immediately the number is from the hospital.

"YO, YALL NEED TO KEEP IT DOWN IT'S THE HOSPITAL!" Nomad yells. Everyone gets silent as Nomad answers the phone with his eyes close to prepare himself for the worst.

"Hello? Yes, this is Doctor Stewart from Good Samaritan. Is this the next of kin of Janice Greene?" Nomad bends over while still seated in the chair to prepare himself for the receiving news. "Yes, this is her son, Nomad. What's up? Is she okay?"

"I'll need for you to come down to the hospital," the doctor states in a calm tone as the room is filled with built up anticipation. Nomad's anxiety gets the best of him.

"Why, what's up? Why can't you tell me on the phone? Is my mother okay?" He asks as he exhales slowly, "Okay, we'll be down there." Nomad looks to Ricky. Everyone stares in silence. Ricky breaks the silence. His eyes wide open.

"SO WHAT'S UP MAN, SPILL IT?" yells Ricky to his brother. Nomad gets up and walks over to his brother. Ricky goes numb and limp as Nomad gets closer to hug him. Nomad reveals the news while still embraced.

"Ma slipped into a coma," he tells Ricky and he backs off, "Hospital wants me to come sign papers to keep her on life support."

"Well that's good news right?" Ricky asks, trying to hold back the tears while sniffling and looking to Nomad for approval.

"I mean she's not dead? Ma is still alive! She still has a chance."
"Yeah...Yeah. Well, look, I'm going to the hospital to sign these papers," Nomad says as he gives a nod for approval.

"Yo, I'm rolling with you." Speed gears up to accompany Nomad.

Chapter 15:
PLACING IN THE
PIECES

"I realize this has been an emotional rollercoaster day for you and your brother; we're doing everything we can do maintain her stability," Doctor Stewart empathizes. Nomad signs the papers in the office with the doctor.

"Thanks. I know, Doc, and my brother and I are highly thankful for everything you have done."

"If there's anything else that comes up, I'll let you know," Doctor Stewart assures Nomad. He reaches over to shake Nomads hand. Nomad and Speed leave the office but the doctor rushes to get their attention.

"Oh, by the way, she's been moved to the shock trauma unit now. She's not allowed any visitors right now until her condition improves. Hospital rules. I don't make them; hope you understand?" Nomad nods.

"Yeah, I understand, and thanks for the heads up."

While walking down the hallway, Nomad makes conversation with Speed.

"Hey, I just remembered. That card is still in my mother's room and I need to go get it," Nomad recalls leaving the card from the henchmen when Speed gives him a concerned look.

"Yo, you sure you're up to it?"

"Yeah, I'm sure," Nomad tells Speed, looking confident but feeling unsure. Making their way to his mother's used-to-be-occupied room, Nomad pauses before he enters the room. He scans the empty room with Speed with assisting him in the search for the card. Speed walks over to the window still looking and scanning. He looks down, noticing a card and bends down to retrieve it.

"Yo, is this it?" He asks Nomad and reads it, "Yeah, this gotta be it." Nomad turns and reaches for it.

"Let me see," He asks and he looks at it and agrees, "Yeah, this it." Nomad's eyes glance at Speed while reading the card. Nomad falls into a deep thought.

> *"IF YOU WASN'T GOING TO BE AT MY FUNERAL, YOU COULD HAVE AT LEAST PAID FOR IT. YOU GOT THE FUNDS TO COVER IT.*
>
> *LOVE STORM"*

At the bottom of the card was a phone number and listed in quotes is, "CALL ME". After Speed finishes reading the card, Nomad responds.

"Whoever wrote this drew some type of connection between me and Storm." Speed, sounding frustrated.

"Man, you can't be serious? Damn! This woman is dead and still causing drama. How can this happen? Are you sure she is even dead?"

"I'm sure, I was there. But before I know what I'm dealing with here, I want to hold off in making this phone call," Nomad tells Speed, sounding positive. Nomad's friend reaches for the card and snatches it from him.

"Fuck it, give it to me, I'll call them!" Nomad smiles.

"Go ahead!" Speed takes out his cell phone and begins dialing.

"They ain't got shit on me! I'll take these mother-fuckers on," Speed rants as he looks at his cell phone.

"Fuck! I forgot I ain't got no more minutes." Nomad smiles and shakes his head.

Speed sounding frustrated, "Damn, I forgot to put some down on it earlier. With all this action going on it slipped my mind." Nomad snatches the card back.

"I know I tried calling you on it earlier. Thank you, now like I said, let me think about this for a minute."

Speed reminds Nomad, "Don't wait too long; no telling how much time they giv'n you to contact them."

"Yeah I know; I'll call them when I get home."

Nomad takes his cell phone out to call his girlfriend and says, "Hey, Baby, I'll be home in a minute. Yeah I'm fine. I'll fill you in when I get home."

Chapter 16:
READJUSTING THE PLAN

Nomad pulls up to the house on his motorcycle into the driveway. Sherri runs to greet him while he is still unmounting his motorcycle in the driveway. Sherri reaches out to hug him.

"Oh my God, are you okay?" Nomad takes off his helmet with one hand and hugging her with the other arm and greets her back with a kiss on the lips.

"Yeah, Baby, I'm fine."

They walk arm in arm to the house. Nomad lays back on the couch. She sits beside him, prompting Nomad to lay his head on her lap.

"You look like you been through hell and back," Sherri says as she massages Nomad's head.

Nomad sighs, "Aaaahhhh.... Baby, you don't know half of it."

"Your brother filled me in on some of it," she says still massaging his head smiling.

"Yeeeeaaahhh Ricky...." Nomad pauses, jumps up and says, "Lookout Baby, I need to take a shower." Sherri throws her hands up to clear his path.

"Damn, Baby, you just got home! Why don't you just relax?!" Sherri fusses as Nomad makes his way to the stairs tiredly. He turns to her with a smile and winks.

"I didn't say I wanted to take a shower alone."

They hold hands walking up the stairs, as they pass a lighted candle. They both make their way into the shower. Nomad caresses her body from behind before getting into the shower.

Nomad and Sherri lie in bed with his arm laying over her with her head on his bare chest. Sherri looks up and turns her head his way.

"Baby, you haven't said much of anything," she says looking at him, "Talk to me." He looks into her eyes deeply.

"It's so much going on; I don't even know where to start."

"Wherever you want to start, I'm here for you." Nomad kisses her on the top of her head softly.

"I know, Baby. Thanks for being there for us. I shouldn't have given up on us so easily a while back."

"And what?" she asks playfully teases him with a seditious smile while laughing. Nomad turns his head feeling almost embarrassed to say it. "Go ahead and say it, come on."

Nomad, like a kid, gives in, "Yeah….and I'm sorry." They play wrestle around in the bed, then he stops and pauses. Sherri turns to him, concerned.

"What's wrong, Baby?"

"I'm not going to give up. I know it's not in…"

"Sherri listen, I hear what you're saying, but I have to pay these hospital bills and it's the only way I know how make that kind of money that fast legally."

While still holding him, "It's gotta be some other way, we just haven't thought it through yet. She kisses him on the lips.

"It's not in my hands anymore. With Ma's cost to stay alive just tripling due to her being on life support. You know, Baby, I been thinking." Sherri sits up and looks at him.

"Yeah, what's that Baby?" she asks while Nomad's rubbing her shoulders.

"I'm going to let the shop go and possibly sell the bike." Nomad turns his head away from her as a look of surprise and hurt falls upon Sherri's face.

"What! Nomad, you joking right?" Sherri takes her hand gently gripping the bottom of his jaw and turning his face very slowly. "Please say you're playing."

Nomad drops his head and sighs, "I'm sorry, Baby, I wish I was." Sherri shakes her head.

"No, I can't let you do that. You have been through too much to just let everything go like that and your bike too. Oh my God, you were the one that started the bike club "Hell Raisers" and you're gonna just turn your back on them like that? No…," Sherri shakes her head and continues, "uh uh…" Nomad jumps in.

"Sherri listen, I hear what you're saying but I have to pay these hospital bills and it's the only way I know how to make that kind of money that fast legally." Sherri lays on his chest and holds him tightly.

"It's gotta be some other way, we just haven't thought it through yet," Sherri assures Nomad as she turns her head up to kiss him on the lips again.

Chapter 17:

NEAR MISS AT THE FASHION SHOW

Pictures from the flashing bright lights of cameras at all angles are captured as people get out of their cars to walk the red carpet onto the Fashion Show floor. A loud roar from an engine of a Corvette is heard pulling up. The photographer's flashes are now focused on the Corvette. From the rear of the car, at ground level, the driver's side door opens and the audience and spectators gasp and whisper to each other in awe as they are mesmerized by her beauty.

A reporter and commentator yells out to trying to get her attention for a mini interview.

"IVY", the reporter calls hurriedly, trying to get the microphone close to the scene, "Ivy, why did you come back? Where'd you disappear to? Are you going to be in the show? Did you and Ti'arra-M, team up as planned a year ago?" Ivy looks at the commentator while waving to her admirers and replies.

"No comments. Just enjoy the show. I know I will." Ivy makes a quick departure onto the red carpet draped along the walkway entering the hotel, making a quick entrance into the Fashion Show. Music is played loudly and heard by the DJ on the Fashion Show floor.

Ivy makes her way to the dressing room. As Ivy swings the door open with authority, her presence disturbs the atmosphere in the dressing room and is quickly felt through the reaction of models and makeup artist.

"Com'n, Tony, pick man, pick up!" Drew yells excited. Tony's answering service comes on. Drew is in the car making his way around the parking lot looking for a place to park.

"Damn! Yo, Tony, I'm down here at the Fashion Show and that Vette is here. I'm going in! Hit me back!"

Now even more anxious, Drew's fussing aloud and frustrated, trying to find a parking spot. Drew sees a parking space.

"Yeah, let's see what's really up?!" Drew yells out loud to himself.

~   ~

"Well, well", Ti'arra-M says while folding her arms, "Look what Hurricane Katrina just blew in here!"

"Who's that?" The model says looking confused and curious. Ti'arra-M responds.

"Her twin sister." Ivy says holding her hands on the hip leaning to her right side.

"It's nice to see you too." The model is now more confused and more curious.

"Oh, you two know each other?" Sarcasm fills the air and Ti'arra-M is sterner than ever.

"Oh yeah, we shared a common interest some time ago."

"You still on that trip? Why can't we just leave the past where it is? Come on, Ti'arra, there's no way you could have thought that you and Brian were going to make it. He wasn't your type," Ivy tells her nonchalantly while the model looks over to the makeup artist.

"Ooooooohhhhh, girl, this is getting good!" Ti'arra gives her a look of mind your business.

"Look Ivy, I'm a better woman than that. I know you didn't come out of hiding to find me to tell me that? Ivy idles her own attitude.

"Your right. "Look, is it somewhere else we can talk?" Ti'arra looks at Ivy, points at another door and gets up towards it giving her a gesture to follow.

"Yeah, in here." Ivy says as she follows and the door shuts. Meanwhile, inside the fashion show, Drew makes his entrance into the Fashion show. The DJ makes an announcement for everyone to sit back and enjoy the show created by Ti'arra-M and the audience applauds. Drew finds the most advantaged place in the room to keep the Corvette and audience in view. The fashion show begins as the models approach the runway capturing all angles of models conducting their stop and pose position.

Drew stares at his watch and glances back at the Corvette. The audience applauses while admiring the

.fas

fashion designs. Drew's cell phone rings and he answers his cell phone. Drew is hasty.

"Where are you man? I've been calling you?"

"Yeah, I know. Sorry. I'm about 15-20 min out. Is the Vette still there?" Tony says trying to calm Drew down. Drew does a quick glance around.

"Yeah, but no signs of anyone taking ownership of it."

"Damn, this could take all night," Tony pauses, "hold on, I got an idea. I should have thought of this before. Drew go out and read the tag number to me."

"Read you her tag number? What you're a psychic now and gonna tell me what she looks like?" Drew asks confused and looks at his cell phone. Tony gets a little irritated with his response.

"No, I'm going to send it to Denise for her to run the tags." Drew goes outside while still on phone and mutters.

"Denise…Denise wasn't she one of our account-ants? Hey didn't we fire her a couple years ago for computer hacking on the job?"

"Yeah we did. I stayed in touch with her off and on, she was fine, I kinda liked her," Tony says still driving. Drew makes his way to the rear of the car to read the Tag numbers.

"We fire her and then you try to get with her? OK, Tony, I got the tag numbers. Are you ready?"

"Okay Shoot!" Tony tells him ready to copy.

"Alright, L - T - D - 1 -2- 4, Duval Florida?"

"Got it."

"Why did she come all the way from Florida to see Storm if Storm was with D?"

"I don't know but I'll run her tags and get back to you. Keep your line open."

"OK cool," Drew responds as he closes the cell phone. Tony dials Denise number and it rings. She picks up.

"Hey Beautiful!" Denise looks at the phone.

"What do you need this time Tony?"

"Hmmm, I must be losing my charm with you."

"And I must be losing my patience with you. When you gonna put in that word for me at the firm? This little cheesy job I have now ain't doing it."

"Baby, you know I'm going to look out for you but first I got a "big fish" to fry. Are you hungry?" Denise smiles and responds.

"Always, what's the cash prize worth?" Tony boasts.

"Well that depends on the appetite. I need you to run a license tag number for me. I don't have much time.

"Ooooh, Tony, I don't know. DMV just installed a new fire wall that tags any unknown signature trying to get in and traces it right back to its origin. It's too risky." Tony throws a bone.

"$3,000.00. Say you get through that fire wall un-detected." Denise begins hacking through Drew and Tony's account at the company.

"You know, Tony, looking at your companies ac-count, I'd say you could up the ante on that offer. But I'll be happy with $6,000.00." Tony is caught off guard.

"What? $6,000.00? Denise, if you don't get out of my account! Who do you think I am, Donald Trump?"

"Do we have a deal?" Denise asks as she looks at her phone. Tony slams his hand on the steering wheel.

"Looks like I don't have a choice. Ok here's the tag number L - T - D - 1 –2- 4, Duval Florida. Do your thing, Baby, and call me back."

~   ~

Ivy and Ti'arra are in the room still talking. Ti'arra is leaning on countertop with arms folded. Ivy mentions Storms sudden death to Ti'arra. Ti'arra sounding irritated replies.

"Yeah I heard. Did you have anything to do with that?"

"Of course not!" Ivy explains, "I came to Baltimore to rescue her. She sent a text saying she needed my help in getting out of Baltimore. She said "D" was tripping and was up to something and..." Tiarra cuts Ivy off.

"And here you are."

"Yes here I am." Ivy says sounding concerned.

"You know, Ivy, you were never one to be concerned with helping anyone unless it was something in it for you so why are you really here?" Ivy reminds Tiarra of their past together and how Storm, Tiarra and Ivy met during fashion modeling school in their late teens. They all made a pact to stick together and own their fashion design label. As the years went on, their life experience with love and pain began hindering the expectations to achieve that goal. To begin, Ivy took an interest in Ti'arra's boyfriend, Brian, and they both began their quest to have an affair behind Ti'arra's back. Needless to say, the passion Ivy and Brian displayed finally surfaced and could no longer be hidden from Ti'arra.

After revealing this to Ti'arra, Brian and Ivy headed to Jacksonville, Florida to get a brand new start. Ti'arra moved forward with Fashion Designing and owning her label. But before Ivy left Baltimore, she tried to convince Storm to go with her and Brian. Storm refused due to her encounter in meeting someone new (Drew) and felt it would have been a bad move to just up and leave. After being married to Drew for over a year, Storm became bored and left Drew and began venturing back to the life she was used to. Ti'arra is trying to make sense of Ivy's situation.

"So let me understand this. You need my help to get you and Brian, not to mention the man I was in love with, out of this mess!"

"Ti'arra, I wouldn't be asking you this but our lives are literally in danger. You think it's this easy for me to humble myself asking you for this help?" Ti'arra goes to explain.

"You know when you used to model for my shows awhile back, I saw the high potential you had," Ti'arra points to herself, "I took you under my wing and was going to make you my business partner. But no, that wasn't good enough for you. You wanted more; my business and my man. Well out of the two, you got one."

"Okay, okay, Ti'arra, I was wrong! Is that what you wanted to hear?"

"How much are you two in over your heads anyway?" Ivy responds in a very low tone.

"$200,000.00…"

"WHAT! 200 GRAND?" What the hell? What y'all dealing drugs now and got caught up? What the hell were y'all thinking?" Ti'arra repeats surprisingly.

No it's not like that at all. Brian and I borrowed some money from some people. "Quick Cash" is what they call it to start our own line of work; well the business didn't do well and ..." Ivy tells her as she shakes her head.

"And now they want their money back with interest," Tiarra interrupts abruptly. Ivy exhales.

"Yeah...," Ivy pauses, "Can you please help us? We'll pay you back. I promise!"

"Ivy, my finances are tied in with investments. I would have to liquidate some of it to get that kind of money," Ti'arra says in an empathetic tone.

"So you saying you would help?

"No I didn't say that."

"Then what are saying?" Ti'arra smiles wide.

"I'm saying there's a big storm in the forecast; you and Brian need to run for shelter quick."

"I see. I told Brian that you wouldn't lend a hand. Brian had wanted you to have this; told me to give it to you and for you to forgive him," Ivy responds, sounding furiously disappointed.

Ivy slightly turns her back to Ti'arra and reaches into her purse. The handle of a hand gun is revealed and the door opens suddenly. The make-up artist interrupts.

"Ti'arra, you are on girl! Come on, let's go." Ti'arra gives Ivy a hug as she's about to leave.

"I gotta show to do. You want to give it to me now or later after the show?" Ti'arra asks as she holds out her hand.

"No, I'll give it to you later," Ivy says with the seediest smile. Ti'arra turns to exit with Ivy following close behind her. Ti'arra turns her head back to Ivy and they begin talking the same time.

"Okay, fine by me. You know I'm throwing an after party at the Sheraton Hotel Ballroom. You're invited to come if like." Ti'arra and Ivy walk out through the rooms and passes a coordinator using a computer laptop. He waves to Ti'arra and tells them to knock 'em dead. The coordinator continues typing away on the keyboard.

Denise hands punch the keyboard, hacking away, as she breaks through the firewall successfully. She dials Tony. Tony's cell phone rings.

"Please tell me you got something." Denise swings around in her chair.

"For $8,000.00, you bet your sweet ass I do." Tony raises the tone in his voice.

"WHAT? Denise, we agreed $6,000.00." Denise, with a smile, handles Tony.

"Whooooaaa, well you looky there! The stocks just went up to $10,000.00," she says as she leans forward toward the desk at the computer screen.

"Do we have a deal or not?"

"Alright –alright! Damn girl, you are dangerous. Ok give it to me." Denise gets closer to the computer screen on the desk and swivels slightly back and forth.

"OK. Her name is Ivyonce Nicole Anderson. She lives on 1024 Deer Lake Drive, Jacksonville Florida, very pretty, and she's definitely your type. Go get'em playa-playa." Tony repeats the name.

"Look, can you shoot that picture to a cell phone?"

"Sure! I'll have to download it to my cell phone then I'll shoot it to you. Is this the number where you want it?" Denise sounds off with victory.

"Yeah, no hold it. Shoot it to 555-736-0028." Tony says, eyes shifting around while driving. Denise types on the keyboard.

"Ok, give me a few and it will be there. Oh and by the way, Tony, you haven't lost your charm with me."

"No, but I lost a lot money to you," Tony responds. Tony looks at his cell phone and begins dialing Drew. Drew is leaning against the wall, being bored, and still taking glances at the parked Vette when his cell phone rings.

"Man, it's about time. What's up?"

"OK. The woman's name is Ivyonce Nicole Anderson," Tony explains as a frown falls upon Drew's face.

"Oh that's good, Tony, now how do I match a name with a face?   I still don't have…" Drew tells Tony as he laughs.

"Technology, my Brother. Denise is down loading her picture and should be shooting it to you in a second."
"Damn, she's that good huh?" Drew tells Tony, impressed.

"Better…oh by the way, we're going to be $10,000.00 short in our account." Drew is confused.

"$10,000.00 short? Huh? What are you talking about Tony?" Drew questions as Tony is trying to think of how to tell Drew later.

"I'll…. aahhh…explain it to you later but…" Drew interrupts and hears an alert on his cell.

"Hold on…" Drew tells Tony as he looks at his cell phone.

"Tony my battery is getting low; I need to go."

"OK. I'll see you in a few."

Ti'arra and Ivy are exiting the dressing room, making their way into the crowd. The audience cheers them both on and Ti'arra parts to make her way to the runway stage to get her props as Ivy makes her way to the exit. Ivy stops, turns and looks at the stage watching Ti'arra on stage waving to her fans.   The audience stands to give their applause. The DJ chips in with an introduction.

"LADIES AND GENTLEMEN, I NOW GIVE YOU THE FINEST FASHION DESIGNER OF THE CENTURY! TEEEEEIIIAAARRRAAA–MMMM"!

Ti'arra is on stage still waving. Flashes from cameras are blinding as they multiply by the second. Ivy still stands a few feet from the stage admiring Ti'arra's moment with Drew on his cell just a couple feet away behind Ivy. Drew is holding his cell watching his phone go through the download phase for receiving a message with an attachment. Upon completion, Drew begins a massive Manhunt, holding his cell phone trying to be discreet in keeping it close to his self; waist level and looking forward and down at his cell phone.

As Ivy turns around to make her hurriedly exit, Drew has shifted directions in his search and accidently knocks Ivy's purse from her hand causing Drew's cell phone to fall from his hand and slide across the floor revealing the phone still on displaying Ivy's picture on it. The picture fades away because of the low battery.

Ivy quickly stoops down to retrieve a few items that were knocked on the floor. Ivy stoops down retrieving her items with a slight quarter turn away from Drew with a truly frustrated attitude.

"Really? Brother man, can you watch where you're stepping?"

Drew is truly apologetic and attempts to assist her really fast but she refuses and waves him off.

"I'm so sorry Miss my bad." Ivy waves her hand to gesture him off.

"Look, just go, I got this, you done enough." Ivy continues out the door and exit. Drew does a quick visual scan to locate his cell phone and retrieves his cell phone and in frustration turns it back on and it rings. Tony makes his approach just outside on his cell phone and passes Ivy just as she exits. Tony opens the door for Ivy and Tony makes a friendly hello and she nods a hello back to him while she continues on her way. Tony approaches the entrance while on cell phone with Drew.

"Drew, I'm just making my way into the Show. Did you get the picture?" Drew looks around.

"Yeah! Where are you?" he says waving his hand, "OK, I see you." Tony closes his cell phone and walks over to Drew. Drew and Tony engage in the ritual hand shake and hug. Drew's still holding his cell phone while the picture re-downloads. Ivy makes her way outside and walks around to the driver's side, frustrated, trying to find the keys. She is frantically looking and shaking her purse around for the keys and fussing aloud. Ivy finds the keys and takes a deep breath as she uses the remote to unlock the door. Drew looks around and Tony looks at Drew's cell phone.

"Good to see you man, is this the picture of her?" Tony asks as his cell phone finishes the download. Drew has a flashback of bumping into Ivy and puts it together. He breaks for the exit and yells.

"SHE WAS JUST HERE"! Tony runs behind Drew.

"WHAT! ARE YOU SURE?" Tony asks just as Drew and Tony approach. Rushing to the exit, they get a view of the rear of the Corvette spinning off. Drew points to the Corvette as the car takes off and throws his hands in the air. He then looks to Tony.

"Now ask me that question again? AM I SURE?" he says walking around in a mini circle trying to recollect his thoughts.

"Damn, we almost had her." Drew shows Tony the phone. Tony retrieves the cell phone from Drew.

"Aww man, I just saw her too Drew. On my way in, I walked right by her and spoke. Damn, I'm sorry man." Tony sighs as Drew drops his head, places his hand on his side and looks to Tony.

"That's all right man. We got it once, we'll get it again"

The city's street night lights shine a brilliant light of a face of a digital clock displaying 10:37pm in the bedroom. Nomad and his girlfriend lay in bed hugged up sleep. Nomad checks to see if she's asleep as he turns his head. He gets up slowly trying not to wake her. He gets up and retrieves the card from his back pants pocket. His jeans lay across the chair while he retrieves the card from the pocket. While on his way out the bedroom, he retrieves his cell phone and heads towards the stairs. Nomad makes his descent down stairs. He looks back upstairs to ensure that he doesn't hear any movement and finds a spot in the living room that will minimize talk chatter noise while on the phone. He dials his Brother Ricky.

"Hey Nomad, what's up?"

"Checking on you. What's that noise in the background?" Nomad asks in a hushed tone. Ricky is concentrating on his hand he was just dealt.

"Just playing cards with some of my boys trying to clear the mind -you know what I mean?" Nomad smiles and nods.

"Yeah, I know what you mean but playing cards wasn't in the plan for me," Nomad tells his brother as he looks upstairs and smiles.

"Did you get to see Ma?" Ricky asks hesitantly.

"Naw, they had her in some restricted room where you can't see her. You know hospital rules. Hey sometime tomorrow, I need to see you to talk to you about some things, OK?" he tells Ricky. Ricky acknowledges.

"Oh, Okay. Damn, almost forgot. I was going to call you on it tomorrow, but you just reminded me. You know we all get together every Sunday at the Track to race right?" Nomad interrupts.

"Yo man, I ain't feeling that tomorrow. I need to chill and take care of some business."

"Naw, man, listen, the Bike Club is hosting something special for us there. They wouldn't tell me what it was but made me promise that you and Sherri would be there." Ricky says trying to convince his brother.

"I don't know Ricky I'm just not feeling it." Nomad says shaking his head.

"Come on man, we owe each other a nice little something-something. OK, if you don't want to do it for yourself, show up for me," Ricky tells him, still trying to sell him on going.

"Alright, only for you I'm doing this. Text me the details," Nomad tells Ricky shaking his head. Ricky starts texting.

"Doing it now, cool. So I can count on you and Sherri being there? Right?"

"Yeah, I said I would. I just got the text on the location and time. Ok, I'll catch up with you tomorrow. I'll holla...Peace..." Nomad says as he closes his cell phone. He looks at the card once again, picks it up and begins to dial the number. He looks up at the ceiling and listens to see if Sherri is awake.

Tony watches Drew vent out and Tony's cell phone rings. He looks for it on himself and doesn't recognize the number but answers.

"Now who could this be?"

"Yeah?" Nomad puts on a stern voice, "Yo, I believe you left me your calling card!"

"I'm sorry, I didn't catch the name?" Tony says really confused and still does not know who he's talking to.

"THEY CALL ME NOMAD." Tony breaks away from the entrance of the Fashion Show.

"Nomad!" Tony says as he signals to Drew that Nomad is on the phone.

"Where are you calling me from?" Tony asks as Drew listens in. Nomad already irritated exclaims,

"From my cell phone, Motha Fucka!"

"Don't upset him!" Drew lip synchs to Tony. Tony signals, acknowledges Drew and continues his conversation.

"Oh, that's really bold, calling me from your cell phone," Tony remarks.

"What's even bolder is you giving me yours." Nomad tells him in attempt to balance the conversation.

"I think it's well established that neither one of us are punks. I'm from the ol' school where we stood toe to toe, man to man. You see the picture I'm painting for you." Nomad's attitude is checked and toned down.

"Okay I can respect that. What beef you got with me? Nomad responds with an easy tone.

"None, I just want to talk face to face. No bullets or weapons; you got my word on that." Nomad doesn't like the sound of that.

"If it's that important, why can't we discuss this now?"

"I'm sorry, I thought we established just a moment ago that real men stand toe to toe," Tony says sarcastically.

"Ok, it's like that huh? Good. Let's say we meet at the race track tomorrow at 6pm," Nomad says feeling his man hood being tested. Tony is still talking to Nomad and gives a nod to Drew.

"I'm already there. What will you be wearing?" Nomad pauses and then answers.

"A red fuck'n ribbon." Tony responds sarcastically.

"You know that's really funny, by the way, how's your mother?" Nomad angrily goes off,

"LOOK HERE, MOTHA FUCKA, YOU KEEP YOUR 3 HORSEMEN AWAY FROM HER!" Nomad brings his tone down and paces back and forth. "I swear to God; you don't know me. I will kill you in your kitchen."

"Glad you should bring that up; that's one of the topics that will be discussed, you know killing people," Tony says edging Nomad on even more. Drew shakes his head no to Tony and Tony signals to Drew that he knows what he's doing.

"Let's settle all this when we see you tomorrow."

"Cool, we will be there by the numbers," Nomad says giving warning. Nomad shuts his cell phone the conversation has awaken Sherri. Nomad turns around and is startled by her presence as she's staring at him. She reaches out to hug him.

"What's wrong Baby? Who were you talking to?"

"Nothing, Baby, I'm fine, just one of Ricky friends acting stupid again that's all," Nomad tells Sherri and he returns the hug and holds her. She playfully tugs for him to walk upstairs with her and he gives in.

"Come on back to bed. I'm missing you." They talk and walk while hugging making their way back to bed.

Chapter 18:
DEJA VU

"Brian, glad you called, my plan B failed." Ivy says frantically into her cell phone as she storms her way through the Hotel Lobby. Making her way to the elevator, Ivy impatiently waits for the elevator. Brian is trying to figure things out.

"Ivy, I'm still in the dark of this plan B you referred to earlier today." Brian tells her as she looks up at the elevator floor about to lose her patience. She exhales loudly and comments out loud.

"What the hell is taking this damn thing so long to get here?"

"Ivy talk to me what's going on?" her boyfriend asks sounding concerned. Ivy starts breaking down in tears and walks away from the elevator to gather her thoughts.

"Brian, I'm sorry. Baby, I tried but it didn't work." Brian tries calming Ivy down and says, "Ivy, pull it together, take it slow and tell me what happened. Ivy begins to talk.

"Brian," she pauses, "Don't hate me, Baby, but…"

"But what? Tell me what happened." Ivy looks up at the ceiling then looks at the floor trying to hold back her frustration and tears.

"I went to Ti'arra's fashion show and asked her to help us." Ivy tells him as she closes her eyes tightly standing by for the wrath from Brian.

"YOU DID WHAT? DAMN IT IVY!" Ivy interrupts abruptly.

"I know Brian I know…." She tells him as she looks at the floor shaking her head no. "I got a little anxious and put our business out there and now I know she gloating about it."

"What possessed you to even think that she would even consider, especially the fact of us kicking it while I was still with her," Brian questions her as Ivy pleads.

"I don't know, Brian, I just thought she still had that soft sister spot for me." Ivy whines as Brian begins to understand.

"And that's why you kept your plan quiet. You knew I would have talked you out of trying see her," Brian tells her and she shakes her head yes and sighs.

"Yeah," Ivy says as she makes her way back to the elevator.

"Ok, Ivy let's get past this and go back to our original plan catching up with this Nomad guy," Brian tells her, trying to build her confidence back. Ivy calms down a bit.

"I'm already ahead of you. There's a bike race tomorrow at 6pm at some race track." Brian builds a plan.

"Okay let's place focus on that. You spot him, tail him, and approach him with some sob story. Add some tears, even show him the emails from Storm so he won't think you're' some groupie and boom, he gives in and donates 100 grand that should hold our word good 'til we get the other half. And you're on your way home. Now tell me if that sounds like a plan?"

"No, Brian, it sounds like a movie," Ivy says with a disgruntled look on her face.

Tony and Drew sit in Tony's car reviewing the events that occurred earlier that night. Drew shares his view on the situation.

"Tony, we need to watch it with this Nomad. We don't know his background or the kind of people he knows," Drew says disturbing him.

"The kind of people he knows!" Tony blurts out as he looks out the driver side window then looks straight ahead. "Drew I think you forgot where we came from. I think you got a little soft while navigating your way out of the streets and gaming your way to high society. Hell, Drew, we invented the game. This Nomad is playing by our rules. Don't get it confused. We still own and call the shots out there but in a smarter way. We don't need to be seen to prove our manhood. In this new era, we operate in "Stealth Mode" and that, Drew, gives us the greater advantage. They don't see us coming nor going."

Drew nods head in agreement.

"Tony, I hear what you're saying but we really need to watch our step on this. We don't need a street war...." Tony interrupts, "and a street war we won't have. I give you my word on that!"

"Then we agree to do this my way. This Nomad sounds too confident and a bit dangerous; more like a loose cannon. We can't afford to underestimate his strategy when we meet up with him tomorrow. We are really getting close," Drew says, selling Tony.

"Hey Drew," Tony looks at the dashboard and out to the streets and then looks to Drew, "Hey look, I'm sorry I didn't mean to..."

"It's cool man, you ain't gotta say it," Drew says as seriousness falls upon his face, "Oh, by the way, you come at me like that again, I will show you how soft I haven't gotten." Drew cracks a smile and they both begin to play fight and talking smack to each other. Drew exits the car and closes the door.

"Alright man, go home and get some sleep. We got another long day ahead of us tomorrow."

"Yeah tomorrow should close out this chapter and then everyone should be able to sleep good from here on out," Tony says with confidence. Tony turns on his music in car.

"You right on that, well I'll catch up with you tomorrow. Oh, one more thing. You made mention of being short $10,000.00 out of the company's account?" Drew agrees with a nod and asks.

"WHAT YOU SAY?" I CAN'T HEAR YOU?" Tony yells and he gives him a dumbfounded look and turns up the radio talks loudly. Tony looks at Drew bopping his head.

"Alright man, catch you tomorrow." Tony pulls off and Drew is left standing on sidewalk and looking on throwing his hands up.

An illuminated digital clock displays the time of 1:14am in Nomad's bedroom alongside Sherri, and all is quiet when Nomad begins to make movements. Nomad's having dreams of Storm fighting over the gun and the gun going off. Storm falls on the floor and then to Nomads reaction, he runs to her rescue. He turns her body over. The heavy fog obscures Nomads view and as the dreamy fog clears, it reveals Sherri's face. Nomad goes into a verbal disparity of grief. Nomad cradles her tightly in his arms.

"I GOT YOU BABY. I GOT YOU. YOU AIN'T GOING NO WHERE". A woman's voice is heard...

"GOING WHERE?"

Sherri wakes up Nomad.

"Baby!" she yells as she shakes Nomad and he wakes up opening his eyes wide gasping for air. While his senses readjust back to reality, he looks at Sherri in disbelief of her presence and quickly wraps his arms around her.

"Come here girl. Damn, you feel good." Sherri returns the embracement.

"Nomad, what's wrong? You kept saying in your sleep 'You're not going anywhere...' Who were you talking to?" Nomad still holding her, lays back massaging his forehead while looking at the ceiling. He glances at her still gathering his thoughts trying to interpret his dream.

"Huh? I don't remember," he tells her looking a bit confused. Sherri comforts Nomad. He lays her head on his chest.

"Well whatever it was you were dreaming; you don't have to worry. I'm not going anywhere." Nomad kisses her on the top of her head.

"I know Baby, none of us are," he says comforting her and himself as he slowly turns to look back to the illuminated clock on their night stand.

Chapter 19:
THE RACE FOR THE TRUTH

It's Sunday morning and the clock displays 9:09am. The phone rings and a hand from underneath a blanket reaches out to retrieve the receiver and answers it with the blanket still covering her head.

"Hello?" Ivy answers in a rough morning voice.

"Good morning, Sunshine," Brian says greeting Ivy with enthusiasm.

"What time is it?" Ivy asks and sighs. Brian looks at his watch.

"It's uhhhh… ten after nine. It's late; you're normally up."

"And your normally sleep, what's up?"

"Well not to put more heat on you but I got a greeting card from our lenders this morning. It was sent along with some roses. I thought it was from you," Brian tells her sounding concerned as she places her other hand over her head and groans.

"Ooooohhhhh my head, what did it say?"

"It says: "HOPE YOU ENJOYED THE VACATION AND NOW IT'S TIME TO GET BACK

TO WORK AND PAY US OUR MONEY". Ivy this is not good. We have to make a move fast to get something to these people. They don't like it when people play with their time and their money!" Brian exclaims.

"I know Brian…. I know. We'll get the money," Ivy says, sighing. Brian pitches Ivy an idea.

"Speaking of the money? You would think that Storm would have just put it in a bank account. It sure would have made this a whole lot easier to get around this using fake ID's."

"Storm was too smart for that; had she dropped $500,000.00 in an account, by the banks procedures, it's automatic protocol that anything deposited over $100,000.00 to send out a notification nationwide to every corporate office and bank of any missing funds of that caliber. If an establishment has a claim out there, the account would have been tagged and put on hold with a follow up on investigation bringing on more unwanted attention and her husband Andrew quickly finding her," Ivy explains to her boyfriend.

"Damn. Storm was really on top of her game! So that's why you drew a strong conclusion that the money could be with Nomad."

"Right! Money that high in value don't just disappear. It's passed on or passed down but never passed over," Ivy confirms, sounding sure of herself.

"Right! I follow you. Somebody knows something or somebody," Brian agrees and now on board.

"Well, Baby, hold it down and most importantly, please watch your back. Don't worry, Nomad will be there I'm banking on that!"

"Yeah me too!"

Later that afternoon…

"I don't know about y'all but I'm geared and hyped up about the race meet! Does Nomad and Ricky have a clue yet of what we are doing for him?" Flash shakes his head no.

"Naaahhhh not yet, at least I haven't said anything to him, unless Ricky told him already what we're doing for him."

"So does anyone have a clue why Nomad wanted us to meet him here?" Speed shakes his head no.

"No clue," Speeds responds as he looks around and leans back places his arms around the back rest of sofa, "I don't know but what but whatever it is, it's got to be big." Flash starts blowing Crazy head up on his last race.

"Crazy, you showed them boys out at the last race. How much you won on that again?

"Mmmmm, about $5,000.00," Crazy says as he looks up. Speed laughs and starts clowning him.

"So tell us how much you really got because we know your girl got about 99.9999% of it." Flash joins in.

"Yeah like the pill? For sure right!" Flash says laughing as Crazy shakes his head.

"See, man, there you go again. See y'all don't understand I'm paying bills and holding it up like a real man." Flash jumps in.

"And giving up most your earnings? Yeah, like a real fool!" Flash shouts laughing even louder. Speed caps it off.

"Yeah, partner, you paying bills and she's holding you down…" Nomad walks in and does the ritual hand and hug greeting and sits down. Nomad explains his motives.

"Alright, check this, remember that number that was on that card? Well, I called it last night and me and "ol" boy traded some hard words; said he'd meet us at the race track today." Flash punches his fist into his open palm.

"Okay so let's do this. We need to put the crew on High Alert and tell…" Nomad interrupts and shakes his head.

"No, I haven't even told Ricky. Look, Ricky, is on edge right now and dealing with a lot. A hint of this would have him lose it; especially the situation that's going on with my mother. It's all good what you guys have in store for me and my brother but the show will still go on. Just keep a close eye on my girl. If things get out of hand, then we break. Here's my plan…."

The gate entrance to race track is filled with vendor stands. Red arm bands are being distributed to males and red ribbons to females that are tied around their wrist who are participating in the motorcycle races. Jacket emblems and people carrying their motorcycle helmets, numerous of group gatherings are everywhere. Devonte scopes out the scene while trying not to stand out when his cell phone rings. He answers it, looks around, making contact with Tony who is still en route.

"Have you guys posted and spotted any signs of this Nomad? Remember he's with a club called "Hell Raisers". Devonte looks around.

"All is good here," he says looking at the jacket emblems, "No signs of Hell Raisers. Jason is at the east end and Maurice is making way to West end. I'm going to the South end to see what comes up down there."

"OK, keep moving," Tony orders giving further instructions, "something should surface soon. I'm about 5 minutes out; remember no guns, no violence. You get something call me."

"Got it!" Devonte confirms.

"Tony. Hey, Tony, I'm en route. Should be there in about 10," Drew says as he answers his cell while Tony gives Drew a quick situation report.

"My boys are there now scoping the place. No signs of the "Hell Raisers" yet."

"Ok. Just tell them to stay clear and report."

"They have been briefed in detail. Don't worry we'll get it right this time," Tony replies.

"I hear you, look, I'll give you a call when I get there," Drew says looking around while driving.

"OK see you there."

Tony, Drew and Ivy's cars approach at the same time to the race track parking lot in separate areas. Ivy parks and gets out of car. She tilts her sunglasses down, revealing her eyes as she gets a sound view of the environment along with some other possible prospects as she's admiring the eye candy that crosses her sight. She gives a quick gesture of approval and smiles. She's distracted and consumed with lust as she makes her way to the gate entrance.

"Drew, where are you?"

"Just got in and making my way around," Drew responds, looking around.

"We'll probably be able to cover more ground separated. But as soon as one of us spots something, we don't make a move until we're fitted."

"I'm with you on that. I'll get a fix on where my boys are," Tony nods and agrees.

"Ok hit me back in a few," Drew says as he closes his cell phone.

A loud series of roaring is heard but no sights of motorcycles. Then a tip of a helmet is sighted just on the horizon of the blistering hot street. Then several tips of helmets start to appear still far away, slowly being revealed. The "Hell Raisers" roar from the motorcycles get louder as the club approaches just on the horizon.

Multiple emblems on the "Hell Raisers" helmets are in good view as the headlights, throttle as well as foot shifting gears along with red ribbons and red wrist bands. The rear of the "Hell Raisers" bikes ride past as they approach the racetrack parking lot. The crew unmounts their motorcycles. Nomad and Sherri unmounts his bike. Nomad takes off his helmet. Crazy walks over to Nomad and gives him a ritual hand and hug. Crazy looks to Nomad and grins.

"You ready to do this?"

"Yeah, let's do this," Nomad tells him returning his grin with confidence. As if almost in a semi slow motion affect, upon entering, Nomad gets Sherri's attention.

"Hey Baby, I gotta go use the men's room. I'll be just a minute. You go ahead. I'll catch up," he motions as he kisses her and signals Speed to stay with her. Flash winks to Crazy and acknowledges.

"Yeah I might as well go too. It was a good ride out here."

"Alright cool, we'll catch up on the track," Crazy says to Nomad and Flash gives the side hand shake. Nomad and Flash make their way to the restroom.

Jason, Devonte and Maurice disperse looking for Nomad. Maurice leans against a structure scoping and Devonte stands by the far end of the race track.

"Tony, any signs of Nomad yet?" Drew calls Tony.

"No, not yet," Tony says looking at his watch. "It's still early, what did your boys have?"

"Nothing yet, but I know they are here, I can feel it." Taking notice of the red ribbons and red wrist bands, Drew looks around. "OK, I'll call you if I sight anything."

"He's toying with us," Tony says laughing.

"What? What do you mean?"

"He's toying with us. When I asked him what he would be wearing he said a "Red Ribbon". Look around you Drew," Tony answers, shaking his head and smiling.

"Yeah I see what you mean. OK it's confirmed. He's here and probably watching us," Drew looks at the bands and ribbons and smiles. Tony looks around trying not to look conspicuous.

"Maybe, but we'll play this one out. I promise no one will get hurt."

"Just tell your boys to be ready for anything. We are on his playground and the rules may have changed a little," Drew responds cautiously.

"Will do."

"I'll make my move closer to the track," Drew replies.

"Got it. I'll hang out here." Drew closes cell phone and glances at the red bands and red ribbons. He gets more curios and asks one of the motorcycle members its meaning.

"Excuse me, Miss, that ribbon ...what does it represent?"

"Oh, one of the members of a bike crew's Mother is in the hospital with Cancer and by wearing the ribbon, it says that your donating a percentage of your winnings to the cause," an unknown female club member tells him. Drew throws in the charm.

"This motorcycle member's name wouldn't happen to be Nomad, would it?"

"Hey is this donation for Nomad's Mother?" the female asks another club member.

"Why, who wants to know?" the fellow male club member asks in a cautious and stern tone. The female club member points to Drew.

"He was just asking who the donation cause was for." The fellow male club member gets up on Drew and sizes him up. "Who you, man, IRS? CIA? MIB? I don't know you! Sound off, what's up?" Drew backs off.

"Hey, man, look I don't know you either. I just want to donate to the cause."

"If you want to contribute so much, why you ain't a member?" the male motorcycle club member questions him, jumping in his face. Maurice hears the commotion and spots Drew needing assistance. He dials Tony and mutters to himself while shaking his head.

"And they told us to keep it quiet." Tony answers.

"Yeah you got something?" Maurice walks in the direction of the yelling while talking to Tony.

"Yeah, your boy Drew is about to get a beat down from some punk."

"Get to him quick!"

"I'm already on it!" Maurice shouts, walking towards the situation and intentionally bumps into the second motorcycle member using that as a distraction to diffuse the confrontation.

"Damn, man, watch where you're going! What you blind?"

"Damn man, I'm sorry, my bad, my bad. I'm just trying to get to this race that's all," Maurice surrenders with hands up.

"Come on, let's go!" shouts the female club member tugging on her angry cohort. The second club member goes about his business while staring Maurice and Drew up and down as he leaves. Maurice returns the stare then looks at Drew.

"You alright?"

"Yeah I'm good. Where are the rest of the Guardian Angels?" Drew tells him nodding his head. Maurice takes out his cell phone, dials while looking around then looks to Drew.

"Oh they're around and close by." Tony answers cell phone.

"Did you get to him in time?"

"Yeah, he had the situation totally under control..." he says as he looks towards Drew and winks with a smile, "Hold on, here he is." He hands Drew the cell phone. Tony is concerned.

"Drew, you Okay?"

"Yeah, I'm fine! Look, just found out that these "Red Ribbons and Bands" are possibly a donation to Nomad's Mother being in the hospital. They donate a percentage of their earnings from the winnings."

"Damn, it's no myth, these club members really do look out for their own. OK, let's refocus and get back to the prize at hand."

"No signs of Nomad or the "Hell Raisers", huh?"

"No, not yet, but keep moving around. We'll find them.

Ivy makes her way around when a figure follows her and she hears a voice call out to her.

"Pretty Lady-Pretty, Pretty Lady, you get around don't you?" The voice tells her. Ivy stops, turns around and smiles.

"I do well for myself and I see you do yours as well."

"So how do you go from a Fashion Show to a Bike Race?" the informant, Chris, asks her. Ivy looks around and smiles.

"Call it fate …mmmmm...I don't know?" she says looking over his shoulders. The informant mimics Ivy looking around.

"I call it looking for somebody."

"What? What? Who that you looking for?" Chris asks throwing his hands up. Ivy looks around her back and around again.

"You wouldn't know if I told you."

"Look here, Pretty Lady," Ivy interrupts and formally introduces herself, "Ivy…" Chris returns the same and introduces himself.

"Chris…. Ivy, my lively hood rides on it. Try me." She folds her arms and looks around suspiciously.

"Okay! His name is Nomad." Chris smiles even wider.

"You know there's been a lot of inquiring of him lately? What he running for the next upcoming presidential race?" Chris quickly changes the subject. "Okay but that's not important, back to what you're looking for. Not only do I know who is, I can point him out to you for $200.00..." Ivy points her finger to him and gets real serious.

"$200.00! YOU TRY'N TO HANDLE ME? Wait a minute, your saying he is here?" Chris gives in a little.

"Okay-Okay $150.00, since you my friend then."

"How about this, you take me to the prize and then talk money," Ivy negotiates tilting her head in thought.

"How 'bout we walk and talk to the race track 'cause I need to place some bets in. A small price for a big favor," Chris re-negotiates.

"You're right. Okay," Ivy says reluctantly.

Tony walks, scopes and spots a "Hell Raiser" jacket and attempts to get closer trying not to be noticeable and calls Drew. Drew answers his cell phone.

"Tony, I was about to call you," Drew says as the cell phone signal breaks up. Drew looks at his cell phone. "Hold on, I'm getting a bad signal from where I am."
"Yeah, you're right but go ahead, I can hear you a little," Tony confirms looking at his cell phone.

"Tony I spotted a couple "Hell Raisers"." Tony smiles. "I got something even better. I spotted Nomad..." Drew is trying very hard to hear through the noise around him and what Tony just said due to broken signals.

"What?!? Are you sure?"

"Oh I'm sure, just hurry and get here. I'm going to stand back a bit. I'm at the furthest end of the stands to the right," Tony replies, nodding his head.

"Call your boys and tell them to stay where they are. Maurice is still here with me. No one makes a move 'til I say so. I'm on my way."

As Drew closes his cell phone, the roar of the motorcycles on the track that are about to race, gets his attention. Exhaust pipes and stationary spinning back tires produce smoke from the friction. Drew is drawn to the excitement and steps closer to the track to get a better view. One of the "Hell Raisers" yell out.

"Get'm Crazy, show'em who still Boss! My money is on you!"

Crazy gives him the thumbs up nods his head. The crowd and spectators going crazy. The signal is a go and the motorcycles take off. Ivy and Chris spectate the race as the motorcycles pass them.

"Damn, this going to be a close race."

"OK, you got your bet in. Now can we look for Nomad?" Ivy asks, irritated.

Chris' attention is focused more on the race and calculating who will win, "We don't have to look, we already found him." Ivy looks around.

"Where?" Chris points, "Right there."

Far ahead on the track, as the motorcycles approach ground breaking speed and pass, Ivy stares in the direction that he's pointing.

"Are you sure?"

Crazy performs the up shift process the throttle with hands and feet process as Chris smiles.

"I haven't lied to you yet." Crazy's console indicator sensors are indicating a malfunction in the fuel line when Ivy points,

"Who's that girl he's with?"

"That's Nomad's girlfriend."

Spectators gasp in a hushed roar as a loud crash and explosion is heard and black smoke is seen from afar. A series of screams and "OH SHIT" is heard. Chris looks toward the explosion.

"What the Hell?

Drew, even more curious, steps out the crowd to try and get a closer look. Sherri grabs Nomad and screams. "OH MY GOD, NOMAD!"

Drew standing just next to Sherri, hears her scream Nomad's name. Drew expresses pure astonishment as an announcement is made over loud speaker:

"CAN I HAVE YOUR ATTENTION PLEASE! CAN I HAVE YOUR ATTENTION PLEASE! WE NEED EVERYONE TO STAND CLEAR OF THE TRACK. THERE HAS BEEN AN ACCIDENT AND THE PARAMEDICS ARE ASKING THAT EVERYONE STAND CLEAR. AS SOON AS ALL IS CLEAR, WE CAN RESUME THE EVENT. YOUR PATIENCE AND COOPERATION IS IMPERATIVE. THANK YOU!"

I'm going to see if I can get a closer look," Nomad tells Sherri, looking on. Nomad and Ricky take off with Drew and Maurice following behind him. Sherri yells out to him.

"NOMAD, BE CAREFUL!" Drew is holding his cell phone while keeping distance while following Nomad. Drew makes a phone call.

"Damn, I'm not getting a signal," Drew looks to Maurice, "What about you?" Maurice looks at his cell phone.

"I'm not either. I'll go and scout out Tony and give him a heads up." Drew nods head and agrees.

"OK, we'll meet up."

Tony is watching whom he believes is Nomad but, in actuality, it's Flash wearing Nomad's jacket. Flash is concerned with Crazy's accident, talking to Speed,

"You going down to make sure our boy Crazy is OK?" Speed looking on where the smoke is.

"No, we stick to the plan and stay put. I'm sure Nomad is already on the scene. Remember, we need to lure them to us."

Maurice makes his way to Tony, sounding a little out of breath, "Tony, we need to talk, quick." Tony looks at Maurice.

"Hey, what's up? Where's Drew?" Maurice catching his breath.

"That's why I'm here, it's a set up." Tony is looking confused.

"What's a set up? What are you talking about?" Maurice shakes his head.

"They set us up," he points to Flash, "that's not Nomad!" Tony sounding surprised and smiling.

"What!" pointing, "I'm looking at him! He's right there. Look!" Maurice explains.

"You're looking at someone wearing his jacket but it's not him. Don't believe me, watch this!" Maurice dials Nomad cell phone and hands Tony the phone. Nomad looks at his cell phone and doesn't recognize the number.

"Yo, who is this??

"I'm a little disappointed you stood me up partner," Tony tells him sounding disturbed looking at the Nomad imposter looking around. Nomad smiles.

"Oh, you finally decided to come out to play, huh?

"No one's playing; we just want answers," Tony re-iterates. Nomad observes the crash site scene.

"We'll settle this later." Tony looks at Maurice and dials Drew and looks to Maurice.

"You're right. Damn, I can't get through, what's wrong with Drew's phone?"

Ivy and Sherri both look towards the crash site. Making conversation with Sherri, Ivy asks a question.

"How bad you think it is?" Sherri looking on to-wards the crash site responds, confused.

"I don't know." Sherri takes out her cell phone to call Nomad.

"Damn, I forgot to charge it." Ivy offers assistance.

"Look, I have a universal car phone charger. You can use it for a couple minutes to get a good charge if you really need it? Sista girl, the walk could help relax you a little. My car is parked just outside the entrance," Ivy smiles, "I'm just trying to help a Sista out." Sherri goes along with the plan.

"Okay. Thanks!" Sherri says and walks away with Ivy.

Nomad and Ricky make their way to the crash site, watching the paramedics just lifting the gurney with Crazy on it and placing him into the ambulance. Ricky looks at Nomad and shakes his head.

"Doesn't look good. I'm going to ride with him. Meet me at the hospital. I'm right behind you. Let me get Sherri and we'll be there," Ricky tells his brother giving him a side hand shake as the ambulance takes off. Nomad, along with Drew, stand just off to the side. Nomad departs from the accident scene and heads back. Drew follows Nomad but keeps his distance. Nomad makes a phone call on his cell to locate Sherri and then calls Speed. Speed signals to Flash that Nomad is calling.

"What's the word? Is Crazy all right?" Nomad walks and talks on his cell.

"No he isn't. It was his bike that took the fall." Speed inquires.

"So what did the paramedics say?" Nomad sounds doubtful. "They were working on him pretty hard. Ricky went with him. I'm going to get Sherri," looking around, "and head on out there with him."

"OK we'll meet up with you. Where are you?" Speed asks sounding anxious. Nomad looks around.

"I'm on the move right now looking for Sherri. I'm going to the bathroom. I'll call you right back."

Ivy and Sherri get out the car and Sherri looks at her cell phone.

"Thanks girl." Ivy returns the same.

"No problem, now let's go back in and see what's going on."

"Yeah, girl, let's go," Sherri agrees in a hurry as Ivy points.

"Hey, I know a short cut. Let's go this way," she points, "It will keep us from going through that crowd."

"Okay," Sherri follows. As they walk, Ivy looks around with Sherri ahead of her. Ivy pulls out her gun.

Nomad, in the bathroom, goes to the sink and splashes water on his face. Before he brings his face up, Drew's reflection is reflected in the mirror. Nomad brings his face up and his cell phone rings. He answers it; not taking notice to Drew's presence.

"Hey, Baby, where you at?"

"NOMAD, THIS WOMAN HAS A GUN TO MY HEAD TALKING ABOUT SOME MONEY THAT

YOU HAVE THAT BELONGS TO HER" Sherri yells, sounding frantic and screaming.

"Sherri? Who has a gun to your head? What money? Where are you?" Nomad calls to her confused and frustrated. Drew stands in the shadows listening when Sherri starts crying.

"Baby I love you!" Ivy snatches Sherri's cell phone.

"Nomad, you have 15 minutes to meet me at the warehouse adjacent to the race track and show me where the money is or your little girlfriend will be joining Storm!" Ivy hangs up, looks at her watch and looks at Sherri. "15 minutes, come on, let's keep it moving."

"What money? Sherri?" Nomad yells through the phone and takes a series of deep breaths. He tries to call her back but no response then rushes out the door. Ivy and Sherri make their way into the warehouse with Ivy pointing the gun in trail. Ivy instructs Sherri.

"Okay, this is good right here." Sherri is scared.

"Are you going to kill me?" Ivy looks at her watch and looks around for something to restrain Sherri with.

"Kill you?" Ivy laughs and makes her way around to the front of Sherri, "No, Baby…" as she takes the nose of her gun and traces the contour of Sherri's face. Sherri looks away. "I'm not a Terrorist. I just want my money."

"I think you have it confused; he has no money. His Mother is in Good Samaritan Hospital in a coma. He's already talking about giving up his tattoo shop to pay hospital bills to keep his Mother alive," Sherri pleads trying to negotiate, "Look if you don't believe me, you can call and ask for a patient by the name of Janice Greene. Or let me talk to Nomad and get down to the bottom of all this drama."

"Or how about this? You could say good night and I'll talk to Nomad and get down to the bottom of all this drama," Ivy says slyly moving behind Sherri.

"What? What do you mean?" Sherri questions turning her head around. Ivy knocks Sherri out with the handle of her gun.

Drew follows Nomad dialing Tony's cell. Tony is still hawk eyeing Flash.

"Drew, where are you?" Drew whispers into his cell phone.

"Look, I don't have time to talk. Have your boys move in on the guy wearing Nomad's jacket and detain him. Just in case Nomad gives me the slip. I think he's just as valuable to this as well." Tony acknowledges.

"Got it," looks to Maurice, "Ok. Call Devonte, I'll call Jason. We're moving in." Flash is getting bored.

"Yo, man, this shit is getting stale! These dudes are not going to show up. I'm calling Nomad." Nomad runs to the warehouse and answers his phone.

"Flash, they got Sherri." Flash is in alert status.

"What? They got Sherri? Where?" Nomad is still making his way around the warehouse.

"At some building next to the race track."

"Okay, we're on our way!" Flash closes his cell phone making preps to leave. "Let's roll, we got to help out Nomad." Speed follows suit.

"Alright, let's roll then." Tony, Jason, Maurice and Devonte close in forming a human blockade around Flash and Speed. Tony makes his approach to Flash and Speed.

"You fellas need to hang out a bit." Flash taken by surprised.

"What the? Who the fuck you guys?" Speed attempts to bust a move.

"Aye you gonna need a tank to stop me!" Maurice slightly opens his jacket revealing his .45 Caliber hand gun and Speed backs off.

"But a .45 is equally as powerful." He looks at Flash and whispers. "This is fucked up!"

"Man, you ain't shit without your piece." (Flash looks at Maurice and throws his hands up.

"What's up, huh?" Maurice shakes his head.

"Nothing and that's what it's going to be."

Nomad finds his way to the warehouse door. Opening the door with caution, he scans each area of the hall. Drew follows closely behind Nomad as he listens for clues to find Sherri. Nomad yells out.

"SHERRI! I'M HERE BABY! GIVE ME A SIGN!" Sherri is knocked out on the floor. Ivy stands in the shadows. Just seconds before Ivy reveals herself, Nomad spots a silhouette of a person in a doorway. Drew makes his presence known.

"You look'n for someone?" Ivy stands fast behind a structure and listens in. Nomad turns around and stands his ground.

"Yeah, I'm lookin' for my girl!" Drew comes back.

"And I'm looking for my money!" Nomad gets irritated.

"Look, I'm going to say this one more time, I don't know nothing about no damn money." Drew sounding sarcastic and truthful.

"And I don't know nothing about your girl." Nomad points to Drew.

"BULLSHIT!" Drew looks stern.

"Yeah, that's what all this is. Let me rephrase the question." Drew pulls out a picture and tosses it to Nomad. "If you know about this, you know about my money." Nomad picks up the picture and studies it for a couple of seconds. Nomad admits to knowing Storm.

"Yeah I used to know her. Why? You PO-PO or something?" Drew shakes his head.

"No, I'm Storm's husband, Drew." Ivy in the shadows, hearing all this and has a flashback of seeing Drew at the Fashion Show. Nomad is getting frustrated.

"So what you want from me, a sympathy card?" Ivy listens in to see how this unfolds. Drew yells and points at Nomad.

"I WANT ANSWERS." Nomad paces slowly back and forth and yells back.

"AND I WANT MY GIRL! Look, we can stand here all night about this or make a move it's your call," he yells out, "SHERRI. ARE YOU HERE?" Drew gets to the point.

"Did you kill Storm and take my $500,000.00?" Ivy still listening in, puts the picture together. Nomad becomes non-cooperative.

"Look I ain't answering shit 'til I get my girl. So tell your boys or whoever to let her go or..." Drew interrupts and squares off, "or what?" Nomad rushes Drew with full force.

A fierce fight breaks out with Ivy watching and standing full clear of danger. She thinks out loud.
"Somebody needs to do something or they will kill each other and I'll never find where this money is." Ivy looks around for ideas and finds a strategic place to stay hidden and fires two shots to the air. Nomad is still tangled in the fight with Drew, and after hearing the shots for a quick second, he refocuses to get Drew off of him.

Nomad gets a lucky punch in staggering Drew and yells out.

"SHERRI!"

Nomad runs toward the direction of the shots fired while Drew struggles to get on his feet and gather his thoughts. Ivy returns watching Drew pull himself together and pats himself looking for his cell. Drew finds his cell phone on the ground that was knocked lose during the fight and dials Tony. Tony answers.

"Drew, what's up? You Okay?" Drew feels his jaw.

"Yeah, lucky bastard slipped one in and got away. Talking about his girl then we heard gunshots and he ran off. I don't know what that was all about." Ivy is close by still listening in.

"Did he tell you about the money or where it is?"

"Yeah said he didn't have it," Drew repeats, sounding confused and looking around, "but you're not going to believe this! I think I know where it is but I won't be able to check it out 'til tomorrow morning. And then I'll finish this out to settle the score with Nomad," Drew says still rubbing his pained jaw.

"But look," Ivy still hiding in the shadows, "I'll tell you about that when I see you. Break off from the "Hell Raisers" and I'll meet you in the parking lot." Ivy makes an undetected quick exit to the parking lot. Tony looks at his watch.

"OK See you in 5," Tony says closing his cell phone. He looks over to Maurice, Jason and Devonte'.

"OK fellas your job is done here, let's break." Flash sounds off.

"Wait, hold on! Let me check on my boy Nomad first, nobody goes nowhere!" he says dialing Nomad. Nomad finds his way to Sherri and opens cell phone to answer.

"Yo Flash, I got Sherri. She's OK. I'll meet you outside."

"OK, cool on my way...." He closes cell phone and makes his point, "Look I don't know what this shit was about but if you bring it this way again you will have the "HELL RAISER" brotherhood to deal with. Now we can go!" He shoves Devonte while leaving. Sherri is still feeling the effects from the head blow. Nomad maneuvers himself to help Sherri get on her feet.

"I got you Baby. You OK? Baby, I got you." Sherri hugs on to Nomad crying.

"I thought she was going to kill me." Nomad comforts her with his words.

"And I would have grown wings and went to heaven to bring you back," he tells her smiling. Sherri notices the bruises on Nomad's face and touches him gently.
"Baby, what happened to your face?" Nomad takes her hand off his face and says, "I'm alright, it's nothing.

Don't worry about me." Sherri rubs the back of her head.

"Damn! That bitch hit me hard as hell on my head," she looks around, "Did you see her?" Nomad shakes his head,

"No, Baby, I saw what I needed to see and that was you." Sherri says in a low tone and fastens her pace in walking.

"Let's hurry up before she comes back."

"Don't worry, I got something for her if she does. We need to get to the hospital and check on Crazy," Nomad warns, sounding confident.

Ivy makes her quick exit to her car. Tony, Drew Devonte, Jason and Maurice on the race track parking lot wrapping things up.

"You guys did good. Thanks. We had a couple close calls there for a minute, he looks over to Maurice and laughs, "But all in all, thanks again for pulling through. Now you guys can go back to living your normal lives again 'til we acquire your assistance again," Tony tells his henchmen proudly. Devonte, Jason, Maurice return the same sentiment.

"You're welcome," and depart leaving Drew and Tony in the parking lot. Tony and Drew analyze the event with Tony sounding doubtful.

"You think Nomad was telling the truth about the

money?" Drew leans against Tony's car and looks away from Tony while responding.

"Think about it." Drew then looks at Tony. "Why would his club host a charity to help him with his mother in the hospital? Hell with $500,000.00, he could have provided her with the best home private care off the scale." Tony is in agreement.

"Yeah, your right." Drew looks puzzled. "But what I couldn't figure out was that he kept mentioning some-one having his girlfriend and shots being fired." He looks at Tony. "Was that your work?" Tony shakes his head quickly.

"No. We were all together, all of us. I gave you my word that no one would get hurt, he smirks laughing, "least to say, I stuck to the plan like you instructed."

"That you did…. Thanks."

Tony looks around and looks to Drew.

"So where do you think the money is?" Drew winks.

"I'll let you know after I get it," he points to Tony. Tony smiles and points back.

"Okay –Okay I got it. Right-Right." Drew walks away to his car, stops and slightly turns around and quotes to Tony. "Well you said after today we would have our answers and we got'em."

Tony smiles, "Yeah we did, didn't we? Man what a weekend!" he yells out. Drew continues his walk to the car.

"Well I'm going to head to the house and chill. I'll call you tomorrow."

Tony waves him off.

"Okay, man, I'll be waiting on that phone call when you got something…" Tony says pointing. Drew points back.

"And a call you will get whether I get something or not." While Drew walks away Tony yells to Drew, "Drew, you sure you don't need me or my boys to tag along? I mean that's a lot of money to be handling by yourself." Drew stops in his tracks and doesn't look back. He smiles and looks up, "Yeah, Tony, I'm positive.

Tony is in his car starting it up, "Don't hurt to ask. Take it easy man." Tony drives off, Drew waves hand up and continues to walk to his car. Ivy in full surveillance mode, is in her car watching Drew gets into his car. Drew pulls out exiting the parking lot and heading onto the highway while Ivy keeps ten car lengths behind him. Ivy places a call to Brian, while following Drew, from her cell phone.

"Hey Baby, tell me what I want to hear." Ivy keeping focused on Drew's car, "I'll tell you what you need to know."

Brian excitedly responds, "Okay talk to me."

Ivy fills Brian in, "For sure Nomad is in the clear. He knows nothing about the money. However, Storms husband tried to beat the hell out of Nomad for him to talk. But it turns out Storms husband, Andrew, thinks he knows where the money is. So I'm following him now."

"I Love You, Baby, stay on it." Brian tells her all in good spirits. Ivy returns the same.

"Love you too. I'll call you later."

Drew pulls up into his garage while Ivy watches from inside her car. Ivy drives by Drew's home and circles around and parks car and conducts surveillance. His living room lights come on. Ivy looks at the time and starts dosing off and on.

"Damn, it's 12:15am. He ain't going nowhere." Ivy decides to leave to return at the crack of dawn.

Chapter 20:
THE FINAL RESOLUTION

Dawn approaches over the city on a sunny Monday morning. People are walking in and out of the entrance of the hospital and a doctor walks through the visitor's lounge. Nomad is sleeping in the visitor's lounge on the couch with Sherri by his side along with Speed, Flash, and Ricky. The glare from the sun rays are reflecting off from objects in the lounge dancing on Sherri's face. She wakes up rubbing her head.

"Man, my head still hurts. I should have had one of those doctors look at it last night," Sherri says as she kisses Nomad on the forehead and gets up. Lisa, Crazy's girlfriend exits the elevator, sees Sherri and rushes over to Sherri and a loud cry is heard as she embraces her with a hug.

"He didn't make it," Lisa cries out while holding Sherri, "They have been working on him all night. I can't go on without him. I need him."

"Yo, wake up, something's going on," Flash says as he wakes up from hearing the cries from Sherri and Lisa. Nomad Ricky and Speed pull themselves together. Ricky looks around in desperation.

"What's up? What's going on?" Ricky asks, looking at Lisa and Sherri crying, "This ain't good!" They all get up and rush over to Lisa and Sherri. Speed can't believe what he's seeing.

"Lisa you telling us our boy, Crazy, is gone?" Lisa separates from Sherri to pull herself together.

"He regained consciousness for a couple minutes then he said for you to keep riding on for him and that he will be there with you riding beside you," Lisa tells Speed sniffling as her voice cracks. The weight of the grief begins to fall upon Flash.

"Nah- Nah- Nah, I ain't hearing this. Nah, we gotta go do something!" Flash walks away from his friends, when Nomad walks over to help bring him down while the rest stay with Lisa.

"FLASH! Hold on man...hold on!" Nomad yells out to Flash and running behinds him. Nomad reaches out his hand, placing it on the back of his shoulder. He stops and looks away.

"We gotta do something," Nomad says trying to talk sense to Flash, "Flash, listen to me. You're right, man, you're right. We gotta do something. And that's take care of each other and look after Lisa and Crazy sons. Look. All the money earned today can go to Lisa. We have to take care of each other. That's what we are going to do."

Flash looks down, shakes his head, and then looks up to the ceiling and says, "This is all my fault. I was the one that recruited him into this bike scene."

"No! Don't do this to yourself. I'm not letting you take the blame on this. He did what he loved best and that was riding and riding crazy.

Flash looks down, chuckles then look at Nomad and says, "Yeah, that's how he got his name!" Nomad cracks a slight smile.

"Yeah, he sure did," Flash tells Nomad as he pulls himself together giving him their ritual hand and hug, "Thanks man." Nomad embraces Flash and recites,

"We ride together….," Flash releases the hug and finishes the sacred vow, "We die together." They lightly clash fist at each other.

"Come on, let's go," Nomad says as he and Flash rejoin their friends in the opposite side of the lobby.

A black Corvette pulls up curbside at a good distance down the street from Drew's residence. Ivy looks at her watch while taking note of any signs of Drew in the house.

"I hope I didn't miss him," she says while dialing Brian.

"Yeah." Ivy says good morning in her own way.

"Wake up, Baby. You ready for payday?" Brian is still trying to wake up.

"Yeah, Baby, of course. Tell me you got it?" Ivy is focused.

"Let's just say I got my eye on it and it's within close reach. Has any more heat been coming down on you lately?"

"No, it's been quiet. Really quiet. I don't know if that's a good or bad thing. But I'm still walking and talking. What time is it?" Ivy looks at the time.

"It's early…very early, it's 6:10 am." Brian rubs his head.

"Yeah…you're back on top of your game." Brian starts to open up a little.

"Was there any doubt?"

"No, but I'm glad you mentioned that."

"Why, what's up?"

"You know I've been thinking… after this is over, about us solidifying this relationship and after all we been through…" Ivy shakes her head and interrupts.

"Brian, your breaking up…I can't hear you. What did you say? I still can't hear you. Look, I'll call you back," she yells closes her cell phone shut, "He's crazy", shaking her head and looks around, "the sex ain't that great, Brian."

Drew's car garage door opens up. Ivy sees the back of Drew's car backing out. Ivy speaks aloud in a low tone.

"OK, Baby, let's go. It's show time." Drew's car rear leading out into the street and turning into the neighborhood street traffic. Ivy stays put until he makes the right at the end of the street, follows behind keeping her distance. Drew's cell phone rings and he answers it.

"Drew, how are you doing, man? Still recovering from that beat down?" Tony laughs, just checking up on him with Drew laughing also.

"Yeah, I'm getting too old for this but it's far from being over."

"Another day-another time, you'll see him again."

"You're right on that, my brother. Oh, we will meet up again. Tony, I gotta go. I'll call you back," Drew says as he arrives at his destination and looks for a place to park as close as he can. Ivy continues to keep her distance as Drew takes a chance and parks illegally. Drew looks at the "NO PARKING" sign and thinks aloud, "Hopefully, this will only take but a minute."

Drew gets out of his car. Ivy notices his illegal parking and says, "OK, Brother-man, do what you do and bring it." While waiting patiently in her car, Ivy attaches a silencer on the nose of her gun and looks around taking notice of activities going on outside. Drew makes his way to the park and memories of him and Storm being together start to become stronger and clearer.

Multiple thoughts overwhelm and race through his mind too fast for his conscious to process. His memories come to a halt when Drew stands in front of a park bench where he and Storm used to come out and just talk and enjoy the nature around them. As he stares at the bench, he remembers himself in the past; watching himself sitting on the bench with Storm and relives the moment.

He remembers how Storm used to hug up against him on their bench ...

"This feels like a fairy tale". Then he would give her a soft look.

"What do you mean?"

Storm would say, sounding really in love,

"Of how you came along and just swept me off my feet." Drew would smile, with charm.

"I couldn't help to do just that when our eyes met."

Then Storm would look tenderly at Drew.

"Drew, I just want you to know should anything happens ..." Drew would interrupt her.

"Aw come on, Baby, I don't want to hear that kinda talk from you... ..." Storm would place her finger over his lips to quiet him while she finished her sentence.

"Just listen, should anything happen to anyone one of us, let's promise that this is where we would come when missing each other. This is where I'll always be. Right here." Drew would nod his head yes and they would kiss...

Drew looks up, "Alright, Storm, send me a sign," and starts looking for clues around and up the trees.

"Come on, Baby, talk to me."

Ivy sitting in her car, looking around.

"Come on, brother-man, I don't have all day!" Ivy yells as she sees a policeman eye Drew's car, "Oh no, not now!" The policeman's eyeing Drew's car because of the illegal parking. He looks down at his watch, looks around then leaves.

Drew continues to survey the area well. He walks behind the bench looking at trees and ground. He takes in every detail of the area surrounding the bench and his eyes quickly notices a carving on the back of the bench. Drew quickly runs up on it. The carving reads:

$TORM 2013

Drew runs his fingers over the carving. He runs his fingers over the dollar symbol, runs his hands over the dirt underneath the park bench and looks around for something resembling a shovel or scoop. He finds a broken coke bottle and begins to dig. He feels that he's touched something and tugs at it but realizes he needs to dig wider. He looks around and finds a medium flat bedrock. Drew digs and a small black bag is pulled from the ground. He wipes his hands on the side of his pants and unzips the bag. He opens the bag slightly. Drew looks around cautiously before reaching his hand in the bag and pulls the money half way just to confirm his curiosity. He feels around inside and discovers an envelope sealed in a zip-locked bag, opens the envelope and pulls out a card.

Andrew opens the card and his eyes catches Storms wedding rings fall to the ground. Drew retrieves the rings and begins to read the card:

"DREW, IF YOU ARE READING THIS CARD, IT'S TOO LATE FOR ME. AND YOU REMEMBERED WHAT I SAID ABOUT REFLECTING BACK TO WHAT I TOLD YOU WHAT TO DO WHEN WE MISS EACH OTHER AND EVENTUALLY DISCOVER WHERE I HAVE HIDDEN THE MONEY. FIRST, I WANT TO APOLOGIZE FOR LEAVING YOU. YOU HAVE BROUGHT ALL THE JOY A WOMAN COULD EVER ASK FOR AND I FELL SHORT IN MY PROMISE TO RETURN THE SAME. PLEASE FIND IT IN YOUR HEART TO FORGIVE ME. I WILL ALWAYS CARRY A PART OF YOU WITH ME. I TRULY LOVE YOU. PLEASE FORGIVE ME. I'LL SEE YOU IN YOUR DREAMS.

LOVING YOU FOR ETERNITY, STORM"

Ivy looks at Drew's car. She takes notice of Drew's return to the car with a black bag and preps to heist the money with her gun in hand. She gets out her car but holds her position. Damn it! A policeman approaches Drew's car.

"Excuse me, sir, is this your car?" Drew looks at the "No Parking" sign.

"Uh, yes it is. I know, Officer, I shouldn't have parked here. But I was only going to be a few minutes."

The policeman responds in a calm tone, "Actually, I was going to compliment you on your car, but since you brought it up." He looks at his watch and points at the sign. "According to my watch, you have 6 minutes to move it." Drew looks up at the sign and notices "NO PARKING 9AM-4PM".

"Oh, yeah," he sighs in relief, smiling.

The policeman takes notes of the dirt on Drew's pants and looks at the bag.

"Are you okay?"

"Yes, Officer, I'm fine." Drew tells him, keeping it cool. He looks at himself and the bag, "Oh, yeah, I left my gym bag by mistake over by the tennis court a couple days ago. I got an emergency call on my cell and forgot all about it. I just came back to get it.

"Damn it, of all the times, a cop, I can't believe this! Brother has got to have an angel in his pocket," Ivy yells, irritated and banging both hands on steering wheel. The policeman bids Drew goodbye while he gets into his car. Drew dials Tony on his cell phone.

"Yeah, what you got Drew?"

"Yeah, Hey Tony I got the money," Drew tells Tony while driving ahead. Tony is excited and surprised.

"You really got it? Damn! You go, Sherlock Holmes! Where was it?"

"It's a long story. I'll tell you all about it. But first, I got a score to settle," Drew says, sounding relieved as well.

"You still trying to get back at that Nomad guy?" Tony asks him while at work sitting on the corner of his desk.

"Now where are you going?" Ivy asks, tailing Drew.

Nomad and Sherri open the front door to the house as they try to regain their composure from being at St. Joseph hospital. Sherri makes her way into the kitchen.

"I'm thirsty, hungry, tired and hurting. Nomad, you want anything while I'm in here?" Nomad sits on his couch and looks back to answer her.

"No, Baby, I'm good thanks." Sherri brings up a series of conversations of Ivy, the race, Nomad's fight all talking while fixing something to eat. He glances over to look at his home phone to reveal messages waiting to be retrieved. He yells to Sherri, while in the kitchen.

"Hey Baby, we got a lot of messages." She makes her way into the living room with something to eat and responds in a nonchalant way.

"Probably my job wondering where I am. Either that or them dang bill collectors." Nomad presses the button to retrieve them:

1st Message: *"Hey Bro, on my way to the track. I take it you're on your way 'because you ain't picking your cell. HOOOLLLLLAAAHHH"* Nomad and Sherri look at each other and say the same time "RICKY".

2nd Message: *"Yo, man, we down here at the Clubhouse wait'n on you. Where you at?"* Nomad and Sherri recognize the voice, Nomad looks away and says in a low tone "CRAZY". Sherri hugs Nomad.

3rd Message: *"This is Doctor Stewart from Good Samaritan Hospital* (Nomad gets closer to the speaker) *in care for Janice Greene, please contact me at your soonest. We got some good news. You're Mother has come out of the coma and is fully conscious. Please give me a call at the soonest."*

Sherri screams with joy and hugs Nomad tightly as they embrace each other. Sherri's voice is uplifted.

"Baby that's great news! Hurry up and call them." Sherri says and Nomad dials.

"I am Baby, I am! Hold on, do me a favor and call Ricky from my cell phone and let him know Ma is OK."

"Hello, Doctor Stewart, how can I help you?" The doctors says, sounding cheerful.

"How you Doc? This is Nomad, Janice Greene son." Nomad says returning the cheerful greeting.

"Oh, yeah! Hey, I see you received my message. Your Mother is fine. She's been transferred to the CCU ward for close observation."

"When can we see her?" Nomad asks, sounding anxious. The doctor looks at his watch.

"In about an hour. We're still running tests."

"OK, we will be there in an hour! Thanks again!" he confirms. Drew drives up into the hospital parking lot and transfers the money into a briefcase. Ivy is still in her car watching him park. She parks not too far from him watching him depart from his car with the briefcase.

"Why is he going to a hospital? Oh no not this time! I'm following you all the way with this one. I'm not losing out on this opportunity," Ivy says thinking aloud.

Drew carries the briefcase, making his way into hospital all while Ivy keeps her distance. Ivy veers off as Drew enters the elevator alone and he presses button number two. Ivy walks towards the elevator, watching the floor read out as to which floor it stops. Drew looks up at the digital readout and elevator doors open. Drew approaches the room only to discover it's empty. He looks at the desk for assistance.

"Excuse me, Nurse, where is the woman that was here a couple days ago?" The Nurse looks at her computer.

"Let's see. Oh, she was moved one floor up Room 314." Drew repeats.

"Room 314." The Nurse comments.

"Yes Sir". Drew leaves the nurses station.

"Thank you", he tells her warmly as he begins to proceed to elevator. The Nurse makes a suggestion.

"Sir, you can use the stairs," pointing to the location of the stairs, "it would probably be faster. I mean it's just one floor up."

"Yeah, you're right. Thanks!" he says as he exits to the stairs. Just as Drew makes his entry into the staircase, Ivy makes her exit from the elevator. She peeps into the first room to open the door. Drew makes his way around looking for Room 314. Drew locates the room and opens the door. Ivy opens up another door. Nomad and Ricky are en route to the hospital.

Ivy checks the last room, opens the door and the Nurse notices Ivy looking into the empty room.

"Excuse me, the patient you're looking for is in Room 314, one floor up." Ivy greets her back with a smile.

"314. Thank you."

Drew sits in the room with Nomad's mother. He sits in a chair slumped over next to Nomads mother, positioned with both hands, rubbing the back of his head with the briefcase in his lap. Drew gazes at Nomad's Mother, barely awake. Nomad's mother, Janice, barely coherent looks over at Drew.

"Who are you?" Drew gives her a slight smile.

"A distant friend of the family." Janice is curious.

"Where's Nomad?" Drew looks at his watch and answers her.

"My strong, educated guess is that he's on his way," looking around, "he should be here soon. Look, I don't have much time but there is something I would like to share with you." Drew holds her hand and explains his history.

"You see, when I was 7, I lost my mother to cancer. I was raised by my Uncle for a very short time which ran the streets and therefore I followed. He taught me the pros and cons for street survival. It was my only way of life so I thought, until the streets claimed him when I was 13. I stayed in trouble with the law and was in the fast lane to being a permanent tenant in jail until I met Tony. We became friends more like brothers. We're business partners now; his family took me in and raised me as their own. His father was into real estate and politics. He showed me the ropes on investing to make money the legal way and set myself up for success. I say all this to...," Drew opens up his briefcase as he reaches into the briefcase. Janice can't believe what she is seeing.

"Oh my God, you can't be serious!

Drew reaching for her hand and placing a couple bricks of cash into it and continues.

"...Give someone else that second chance I had." The door swings open and Drew's reaction is as if he's seen a ghost. As he turns around, Ivy enters the room.

"IVYONCE! WHERE DID YOU COME FROM?"

Ivy quickly takes out her gun and points it.

"I prefer Ivy, thank you! I see you have done your homework, ANDREW!"

Uhum, excuse me, Miss, but can somebody explain to me what the hell is going on here?" Janice asks, looking confused, intervening. Ivy responds in a sinister way.

"I think that question needs to be directed to Drew." Ivy walks slowly towards Drew and Janice and continues her sentence. "What is going on here Drew?" Drew answers to Ivy.

"I see a person in need of help," turning toward Janice trying to clue her with his eyes to press the help button beside her hand, "and I'm there."

"I'm touched," Ivy replies sarcastically and points the gun at Nomad's mother. "Now what would happen if she couldn't use your help?" Janice throws hands in the air.

"Hold on now. Hold on. You can take this back, it ain't worth all this drama. I didn't just wake up out of a coma last night to get a bullet in my ass the following day. Y'all need to take this somewhere else," Janice says, looking at Drew. "Look, it was nice meeting you and…" Drew interrupts and raises his voice, looking at Ivy.

Drew looks to Ivy, cautious of her intentions and says,

"Ivy, you can't be serious!" Ivy points her gun gesturing for Drew to stay seated.

"Ah-ah-ah, stay seated. Drew, you have no idea how serious this is. I'm not letting nothing come between me and my way out this mess I'm in, especially when dead people can't testify? Right?" Ivy says shaking her head. "You should have stayed in your coma."

Janice's eyes are filled with fear as her heart rate rises. Ivy points the nozzle aiming at Janice and fires her gun, with Drew diving in front of Janice to take the bullet. Janice goes into a panic attack placing both hands over her chest with Drew still slumped over her trying to remain conscious while trying to protect her. Ivy rushes to retrieve the briefcase and points the gun at Janice while panicking.

"I'm not going to have to shoot you after all. I can just watch you have a heart attack…" Ivy says to Janice in a sadistic tone. Drew struggles to remain conscious and reaches for the panic help button and presses it. Ivy spots Drew's reaction.

"Shit!" After Ivy realizes what Drew did, she quickly exits as the doctor's rush in when Ivy responds with, "Glad you made it, something's terribly wrong."

Ivy quickly makes her way to the hall way to the elevator and is met by Nomad as the doors open up. They are face to face. Nomad speaks as she enters and he exits. Nomad and Ricky make conversation while walking down the hall and makes a gesture to Ricky.

"When Sherri and Lisa get here, if you're not busy, we can go out and have some lunch. It's on me.

"Yeah you did say you wanted to talk to me," Ricky says, reminding him of a past talk. "314-314. Wait a minute it should be," Ricky turns around and points in the direction of nurses and the doctors running. He looks at Nomad. "Oh no, not again."

Ricky and Nomad rush to the room, and as they enter the room, they see their mother partially in bed assisting the doctors moving Andrew onto a wheelchair. Nomad and Ricky try to piece together what's going on. The doctors and nurses are telling everyone to stay calm and to take it easy. Nomad notices Andrew while the doctors help him in the chair then his attention is grasped by his mother. She musters the energy and yells out to him.

"NOMAD, come here!" The doctors urge her to stay calm. Nomad is still trying to put this all together while rushing over to his mother.

"Ma! What's going on here? Did he try to...?" Janice interrupts and shakes her head no head and grabs Nomad hands talking out of disparity, taking deep breaths.

"Look, no time to explain! There's a woman with a briefcase that just left here! Hurry up and get Security and find her. GET THAT BRIEFCASE! She can't be too far. Now go! Hurry!" Nomad looks at Ricky.

"Stay here with Ma 'til I get back." Nomad turns to gain momentum to run. Just as he passes, Drew says aloud,

"PLEASE GET MY BRIEFCASE."

They trade off stares. Nomad runs to the elevator and looks up at the digital display readout, realizing time is of the essence and thinks out loud,

"THE STAIRS."

As he opens the doors to the stairway, he mutters out,

"HERE I GO AGAIN!"

Ivy is in elevator descending down, displaying the digital floor readout while showing Nomad in his descending stair journey. As Ivy reaches the ground floor, the elevator door opens up and she makes her hurriedly exit out of the hospital.

Lisa and Sherri making their approach on hospital grounds. While Lisa and Sherri are in conversation, Ivy still makes her way on the sidewalk towards the parking lot with her head slightly looking down for her keys. As she finds them, just as Ivy looks up after retrieving her keys, Lisa and Sherri pass Ivy. As both parties reach each other, Sherri and Ivy's eyes meet while still in passing. Sherri instincts quicken and in a series of flash backs replayed in Sherri's head, she remembers.

From a far, behind Ivy, Nomad yells out to her.

"SHERRI!"

Ivy's reaction was a bit too slow to counter attack Sherri's first assault with a tightly balled fist to Ivy's face. Ivy is quickly knocked to the ground with that blow followed a wave of kicks to Ivy while on the ground along with the briefcase being knocked out Ivy's hand. Nomad, just distances away, watch as he is in full pursuit to coming to his girlfriend's aid. As he arrives, he pulls Sherri off of Ivy. Lisa stands off to the side really confused as to what is going on yelling at Sherri.

"GIRL, WHAT'S WRONG WITH YOU BEAT'N UP ON PEOPLE!?!"

Nomad arrives and quickly grabs with a strong hold tightly grasped around her waist.

"Baby, it's ok-it's ok! She's down! Look? See?" Sherri is not listening, still in Nomads grip. They both begin into a spiral motion as Sherri tries to get to Ivy who is still barely conscious. Nomad looks at Lisa and gives her instructions.

"Lisa, shut up and be quiet and take the briefcase to my Mother. She's in Room 314."

"Sure, what's in it?" Lisa asks. Nomad is still trying to calm Sherri down.

"I don't know but my Mother sent me down here after her and it. Hurry, and tell her everything's fine. I'll be on my way." Sherri is yelling and still trying to break his grip.

"Let me go, Nomad. I'm gonna kill that "ho"! That's the one that had a gun to me at the race track," Sherri yells as hospital security arrive on the scene.

The security guard helps Ivy on her feet. Ivy still feels dazed and they ask Nomad a question.

"Is this the woman that fits the description?"

"HELL YEAH, OFFICER! PUT HER ASS AWAY..." Sherri yells out. Nomad interrupts, still holding Sherri back.

"Yeah, it's her Officer." The second security guard searches Ivy while the first security guard holds her and finds a gun. The guards look at each other.

"Yeah, it's definitely her. Ok, let's take her to the security office while the police are on their way." Ivy is taken away.

"OK, come on, let's go." Ivy gains a bit of consciousness and looks around while being escorted.

"Wait a minute! Where's my money? Where's my briefcase!" Ivy screams, trying to struggle with the Security Guard still escorting her away. Sherri yells out to Ivy.

"FILL OUT A CLAIM BITCH!" The second security guard looks at Nomad and Sherri.

"We will need for the both of you to come fill out a statement." Nomad cooperates.

"No problem, Officer, but I really need to see my Mother first; she just come out of a coma and she's in Room 314. Can give me about 15-20 min?

"I understand of course, just be sure to stop down before you leave the hospital." Nomad reaches out to shake the security guard's hand.

"Thanks."

"Are you ok? Was anyone hurt?"

"No one but her..." Nomad replies, with a grin, gesturing his head towards Ivy while the security escorts her away.

"We'll take care of her. You need to go see your Mother." Nomad responds.

"You don't have to tell me that twice." Nomad and Sherri walk towards the hospital entrance. Nomad has his arms tightly around Sherri's shoulders with her head lying on his chest.

"You okay, Baby?"

"Yeah, I'm fine. Why didn't you let me finish kicking her ass?" Nomad assures Sherri.

"Sherri, you did! There was nothing left of her. Damn, Baby, you handled yourself real good back there!" He kisses her on the head. "I always said you had a mean right jab."

"Yeah and if you start acting stupid, you gonna feel what this left jab feels like!" Sherri says playfully as they both laugh, walking into the elevator.

Lisa enters Janice's room with the briefcase and places it down on the floor beside her bed. She greets Nomad's Mother with a hug. Janice smiles.

"Hey, Baby…," she reaches out to hug her, "how are you doing?" Lisa looks away trying to hold back the tears.

"Not too good. But the Club gave me some money to hold things over 'til I can get on my feet." Janice reaches out to hold Lisa's hand.

"Ricky told me what happened and I'm sorry, you know I…" Nomad walks in with Sherri and interrupts the conversation.

"Speaking of Ricky, where is he?" Sherri walks over to Nomad's Mother and greets her with a kiss on the cheek. Janice hugs Sherri.

"Boy, you better come here and show your Mother some love first before sounding off!" Nomad smiles and the ladies cheer him on with a series of "yeah's". He gives his Mother a big hug and kisses on the cheek.

"I'm sorry Ma, I missed you!" She returns the same, still holding him.

"I missed you too. Baby, I wasn't going anywhere; just took a little vacation that's all and I'm back now."

Nomad sits down beside her.

"Now, where's Ricky? I sent him to look after that guy that was in here that took a bullet and saved my life," she tells him, laughing. "Well, what's left of it anyway? Oh, that briefcase belonged to him," she says looking for it. "Where is it?"

Nomad picks it up, "Right here." Nomad turns around as Ricky walks in.

"Hey, Bro, I see you wrapped things up," Ricky says sounding cheerful. He hugs Sherri and Lisa, Nomad smiles and points to Sherri.

"No, she wrapped things up!"

Janice eyes look at the briefcase, "Speaking of wrapping things up, we need to get this briefcase back to him. What room is he in, Ricky?" Ricky points down the hall.

"Oh, he's right down the hall. Two rooms down. You guys are practically neighbors. Janice smiles at Ricky.

"Did you thank him for me?"

"Oh, yes Ma'am, you know we talked for a good minute; he's kinda cool. He's doing OK and he's stable. He got hit in the shoulder but they got the bullet out," Ricky says admirably.

"Lucky for him, huh?" Nomad says in a sarcasm way.

Janice jumps in, "No, lucky for me. Nomad, take that briefcase to him," Janice looks to Nomad. Nomad says in a gesturally tone,

"Ricky, go and give this back to him..." Janice interrupts. Janice points to Nomad.

"No, I told you to do it."

"Ma, I'm not going to his room. Why? What's so important about this briefcase anyway? What's the difference if...?" Nomad says, sounding reluctant. Janice interrupts and takes a stand.

"Nomad, go to his room and tell him thank you! What's so hard about that? The man saved my life and that's the gratitude you have? That's not how I raised you. Now go in there and tell him thank you." Nomad nods his head slowly.

"Okay...Okay..." he stands up with the briefcase in his hand and turns around while silence falls upon the room. Nomad gives a gesture to Sherri, "Come on, Sherri, let's go." Janice places a stronger emphasis in her voice.

"No, I said you go. Sherri, you stay right here." Silence remains in the room as Nomad makes his way very slowly to the door while everyone stares, he looks at Ricky. Ricky stands near the door with his arms folded, taunts him and smiles at him.

"You always said Ma liked you better..." Ricky starts laughing. Janice pushes Nomad on.

"Go on now, besides, I believe you two have a lot to discuss."

"You can say that again," Nomad says in a muttered tone while leaving the room.

"What you say, boy?" Janice asks her son.

"Noth'n, Ma. I said I'm going!" Nomad responds to his Mother respectfully.

Nomad walks slowly down the hall to Drew's room. Drew is in a sling, sitting in a wheel chair, watching TV when Nomad enters the room. He sits the briefcase down by the entrance, not wanting to come in. Drew glances over to the briefcase and looks back at the TV. Nomad comments.

"Shouldn't you be in bed? I mean you could tip over in that wheelchair or something; accidents do happen you know." Drew continues to watch TV.

"Yeah, accidents," he turns to Nomad, "I know they do happen, don't they? Drew looks over at the chair offering Nomad to sit. "Why don't you sit down?"

"Why don't I just stand?" Drew gives in.

"Okay, stand then, and I'll be the bigger man to say this I'm…" Nomad interrupts, sounding disturbed.

"Look, man, I don't want to hear all that. I mean if we could have just talked at the Track…." Drew interrupts.

"Like we're talking now..." Nomad becomes silent. "You see, that's the main problem with society today. No one wants to talk face to face anymore. We got internet, chat lines, cell phones and texting. I see kids today with cell phones having lengthy texting conversations with their parents. We depend on artificial means to settle our differences when we need to go back to reaching out with our hearts and send roses or a card instead of using a keyboard saying I'm sorry or a simple "I Love You". Nomad sits down.

"Damn, I wasn't prepared to hear all that, but you're right. Well, since you brought that up..." Drew interrupts.

"Storm ...right? I know, your brother already told me. Don't worry, I can leave the past where it is. Your story is safe and will not be repeated, I promise. I'm happy to know the truth and now I can go on with my life."

Nomad gets up and walks over for the hand and hug ritual, "Thanks for looking out for my Mother."

"And thank you for helping me to get closure and laying Storm's spirit to rest," Andrew replies back.

Nomad walks toward the door, looks down at the brief case and picks it up. He walks back over and hands it to Drew.

"I believe this is yours." Andrew looks at the brief-case and looks up to Nomad.

"Thank you." Nomad smiles.

"You're welcome. Well, I'm going to head back," Nomad says as he turns to leave. Drew stops him before leaving.

"Hold up," Drew opens up the briefcase and a shocking look of surprise comes over Nomad as he catches a glimpse of the money. Drew takes out a couple bricks, "and I believe this is yours. I mean you're still doing the fundraiser for your Mother right?"

"Yeah?" Nomad says, nodding yes. Nomad takes a deep breath while looking up trying to hold back the tears. Drew tosses it to him as Nomad catches it.

"I promise that it will be used for its primary purpose, to do just that; pay for her medication and care."

Nomad places the money inside his coat jacket and walks to the doorway. He stops and looks over his shoulder while Drew still stays focus on the TV.

"And I apologize for the loss of your Wife... Storm."

A tear falls from his right eye as he continues to stay focused on the TV. Drew wheels himself over to the phone in his room.

"Yes, this Room 310. Is this the gift shop? Yes, I'd like to order some roses and have them delivered to Room 314. Yes, you can bill it to this room. Thank you."

"Hey, Tony, you're not gonna believe this!"

"Baby, are you okay? You don't look like yourself?" Sherri asks Nomad, kissing him and giving him a big hug. Nomad embraces her.

"I never felt better. I Love you." Ricky stands off to the side. Nomad sends a soft "thank you" and sticks out his fist to his brother Ricky.

"Thank you." Ricky smiles and winks. The doctor enters and looks to Nomad and smiles.

"Sorry to put a damper in this short visit, but your Mother needs to take her medication and it will make her a little drowsy."

"I guess that's our que to roll," Ricky replies.

"Yes, I'm sorry," the doctor tells them in a remorseful tone.

"We understand, Doc, we know she's in good hands with you," Ricky tells him confidently while walking over to say goodbye to his Mother and the rest follow suit.

"Hey, man, didn't you say lunch was on you?" Ricky asks his brother as they arrive at the elevator and press the down button.

"Yeah, I did, but we got to fill out the report first." Nomad looks towards Sherri and she nods her head.

"Yeah, we gotta take care of that!" Nomad places emphasis, "After business, then we get our eat on."

"Where do you ladies want to eat?" Nomad asks and looks at Lisa and Sherri. They all begin to give their input and Ricky intervenes.

"I was thinking about "RED LOBSTER" or "PHILLIPS RESTAURANT" down at the harbor!"

They all enter the elevator, turn around facing the elevator and just before the doors close, Nomad makes a comment.

"RED LOBSTER" or "PHILLIPS RESTAURANT"? Do I look like I got that kind of money on me?" Nomad looks directly outward, smiles and winks as the elevator doors close shut.

THE END